WAIT IN THE TRUCK

MM HURT COMFORT DADDY ROMANCE

BLUE COLLAR DADDIES IN THE CITY
BOOK 1

ARIA GRACE

SURRENDERED PRESS

Surrendered Press

Wait in the Truck

Copyright © 2023 by Aria Grace

All rights reserved.

No part of this book may be reproduced in any form or by any electronic or mechanical means, including information storage and retrieval systems, without written permission from the author, except for the use of brief quotations in a book review.

CONTENTS

1

HARRIS

"I think I'm gonna do it." I looked down at my phone again and then back at my buddy James. "She's just so sweet."

James sighed and shook his head. "Good for you. But it's quite a drive. Are you sure there's nothing closer?"

"Not like her." That was true. I'd been on a few local dog rescue waiting lists for months, and Luna was the first dog to be offered to me that I could imagine bringing home. She flunked out of the service dog program and needed to be rehomed somewhere without other pets or kids. Since I was perpetually single and not planning to add any children to my household, I was the perfect match for her.

And she was the perfect match for me.

With her grayish-brown coat and golden eyes, she was an absolute beauty. But she was a thousand miles away. Literally. And if I didn't pick her up within the next five days, she'd be euthanized. "Looks like I'm taking a road trip."

"Have fun." James took a gulp of his coffee and watched a guy pass by on the sidewalk. "I'll hold down the fort here."

"You wanna come with me? We haven't been on a long drive together in...ever." I flashed what I hoped was a charming smile, but he wasn't buying it. That drive was rough in great weather and would be absolutely brutal in the winter.

"And we probably never will." James chuckled and leaned back in the wooden chair. "Thanks for the offer, but I'm on call this week." He looked suspiciously relieved to have that excuse at the ready.

"Technically, I am too, but I think I can get Cort to cover for me. He owes me a few shifts for all the times I've covered for him." Cort and I both started working at the metal fabrication shop eight years ago, but he was still in the partying stage of his life and had missed more Monday mornings than I could count.

Since I was firmly rooted in the *Netflix and chill...alone* stage of my life, I never had to worry about hangovers that kept me from doing my job...and his. Besides, the kind of entertainment I was interested in wasn't something I could find in a dive bar or regular club.

I had to wait for special theme nights at the city's kink clubs to connect with potential boys looking for a Daddy. It always seemed like a night full of possibilities and potential matches, but I rarely met anyone worth exchanging numbers with...and had yet to actually connect with someone who was right for me. Or, just as importantly, who I was right for.

Which was why I was getting a dog.

I was tired of coming home to an empty house. At least a dog would be happy to see me and content to curl up on the couch with me and watch TV. And having an excuse to walk past the gay men's yoga-in-the-park meeting that happened every morning in the spring and summer would just be a bonus.

"Welp, I better get back to it." James crumpled up the napkin and wrapper from the blueberry muffin he'd just inhaled and stood up. "I have some new private contracts to work in before the weekend, so I'll catch you later."

I grabbed my trash and walked out with him. If I was going to pick up a dog, I had some work to do at home. There were a few loose boards in my back fence, and I needed to get her a bed. Maybe two so I could keep one by the couch and one by my bed.

But first, I needed to talk to Cort.

———

Cort and I were on different jobs, so I headed back to the shop to get some projects finished there and wait for him to head back. At exactly four in the afternoon, he pulled up in his company truck with a twenty-foot trailer behind him.

My work was done and I was really just killing time, so I turned off the welder and shed my hood before walking out to meet him.

He was already releasing the tie-downs when I got out there. "Hey, man. Wanna make yourself useful?"

"Why do you think I came out here?" I hopped up on the trailer and started rolling up the straps so they'd be ready to put away. "To help a friend out."

He squinted into the sun as he looked up at me. "Don't bullshit me. What do you want?"

I guess we'd been working together long enough for him to know me well. "You gonna be around for the next few days?"

He cocked his head and shrugged. "Yeah, I guess. Why?"

"Well, I need to go out of town for a few days. Can you cover me if any service calls come in?"

Cort perked right up. "Yeah, of course. I could use the extra hours anyway. I want to take a trip to Germany for Oktoberfest next year."

"That's...random." I handed him the straps and started pushing the metal tubes he was transporting toward the edge of the trailer so we could grab them easier. "But, thanks. I appreciate it."

He grabbed one end of a tube and waited for me to hop down so I could grab the other end. "Anytime. Especially if you help me unload as part of the buttering-up process."

"Well, I'm picking up a dog, so I'll probably need more evenings at home. Which means, if you want the overtime, it's yours."

"Sounds good to me." Cort and I walked inside the warehouse and carefully lowered the tube onto a rack. He patted my shoulder and started walking back to the truck. "One down, seventeen more to go."

I inhaled deeply and followed. "Yeah, you better remember this the next time I have a heavy load to move."

He turned to look over his shoulder and winked. "Yes, Daddy."

It was a running joke between us that whenever one of us got a little bossy, we'd throw that out there. No one at work thought of it as more than a joke, but we knew the truth behind it. And that was what made it funny sometimes and annoying the rest of the time.

I scoffed. "If you were my boy, your ass would be bright red right now."

He chuckled. "Promises, promises..."

2

JESSE

Is this it?

Have I finally found the sweet release of death?

I turned my head and a shooting pain pierced through me from head to toe. Then I realized it wasn't. There was no way death could hurt that badly. The total darkness surrounding me was deceptive at first, but as soon as my eyes began to adjust, I remembered where I was. Crouched in the closet with my feet wedged against the accordion door to keep Bruce from opening it.

Not that he couldn't get in if he really wanted to.

But he was usually so far gone by the time he was done with me, he was probably passed out for at least a few hours. Unless, it had already been a few hours. I had to bite my tongue to keep from crying out as I reached into my back pocket to fish out my phone.

It was just after eight, and he had come home at 6:30. He was already drunk before he started in on a new bottle, so I'd probably only been hiding for twenty or thirty minutes.

But this beating was one of the worst.

They were never good or easy, but sometimes, he would just throw something at me and be done with it. Tonight, he was in a mood and wasn't ready to back down until he physically passed out or killed me. Luckily, he winded himself and closed his eyes just long enough for the alcohol to lull him to sleep.

Which meant this was probably my last chance.

I could try to get away right now, and I'd have a 50/50 chance of survival. But if I were to stay through the night, I might not make it another 24 hours. The way he was waving around his 12 gauge was new. He liked to pull it out now and then just to remind me he was in charge. But he usually didn't press it right to my face and pretend he was gonna pull the trigger. That was also new.

Which meant it was officially time for me to leave.

I couldn't take another night of that torture. I was fairly certain I would die from the cold or whatever internal injuries I had, but that would be better than living with him in constant fear.

It took a while, but I slowly pushed myself up against the wall until I was upright and able to stand. Blood was crusted along the side of my head and dripped down my neck, and when my shirt pulled away from the scab, the cut on my elbow from when he threw me to the ground began to bleed again.

But none of that really mattered. That kind of pain could be ignored. It was the fear that I hated most. Never knowing how he was going to react from one second to the next was not worth any sense of security he claimed to offer me. At first, I had appreciated that he took me in when I was on the streets, but the price of that shelter quickly became way too high.

I would have been better off braving the elements and sickos on my own than agreeing to go with him. But I was desperate and gullible, and when he said he would take care of me, I believed him.

Unfortunately, his idea of taking care of me was much more violent than I had ever anticipated. I pulled open the closet door just far enough for me to peek out and listen. I could hear Bruce's loud snoring from the other side of the trailer, so I knew I'd be okay for a while.

When he was in a deep sleep, nothing could wake him.

As quietly as I could, I grabbed my backpack and shoved some clothes inside. Bruce's wallet was next to the dresser, and I briefly debated whether or not to take his cash, but I didn't want to give him any more reason to hunt me down. Best-case scenario was that he would be glad to be rid of me and forget I ever existed.

But that wasn't realistic.

He would try to find me. And taking even a single dollar from him would just be taunting him to come for me even sooner. With my boots in my hand so I wouldn't make any noise, I slipped past him and got to the door.

The door to his old trailer was creaky, but he had the TV on, so I turned up the volume two notches and waited for some loud talking before I yanked open the door and slipped outside. The few seconds it took for me to step into my boots and start running felt like hours. But I made it all the way to the road without any sound coming from the trailer.

Snow was falling lightly, but the storm hadn't fully rolled in yet.

If I could just put a few miles between us, I had a chance.

At least, I thought I did until the few snowflakes turned into flurries and the wind picked up to the point that I could barely keep my eyes open. I kept walking, hoping a truck or Good Samaritan would stop and pick me up. But there weren't many cars on the road, and whenever a vehicle approached from behind me, I had to get off the road and hide in the tree line. Every passing car could have had Bruce in it, and I didn't risk my life just to let him pick me up on the side of the road.

I kept walking, but as I continued on, the loss of blood and lack of calories started to take their toll on me.

Every footstep became a Herculean effort, and I was sure I'd die from hypothermia before any sort of rescue might come my way.

As I approached an intersection with the highway, I remembered a bus stop to the east. I didn't have money for a ticket, but the news people had been talking about a *Rides for Warmth* program that would allow me to get out of the weather for a couple hours at no cost.

Maybe all I needed was to warm up and then my brain would function a little better. I just needed to be able to think through a plan if I had any hope of saving myself.

It seemed to take a million steps against the harsh wind, but finally, the plexiglass enclosure came into view. Once I was sure it wasn't a figment of my imagination, that box became my singular focus. I just had to get inside and wait for a bus to come along.

I could do it.

Of course, if Bruce came along first, he would just finish me off right there. And there was always the chance that a bus wouldn't come at all, and I would die on the bench. No matter what happened, this was it. I couldn't go any farther on foot, and I had no one to call for help. Even if I had someone to call, I'd tossed my phone into the woods on my way out.

I didn't know if Bruce had any way of tracking me, but I wasn't willing to take that chance.

When I finally reached the bus stop, the tiniest thread of hope filled me. It wasn't any warmer inside the plastic box than outside, but at least I was mostly shielded from the wind. Huddling against the clear wall in the farthest corner, I curled up into a ball. My body had no heat left, but that didn't stop me from rubbing up and down my arms and legs, urging the blood to start circulating again.

The snow was falling hard, and it was clear that my time was almost up. At least I would die trying. For some sick reason, that gave me comfort. If I had let Bruce take my life, it would've been much more painful than how I was going.

As it was, the pain was starting to drift away. My head no longer throbbed. My feet no longer ached, and a general numbness had settled over me as I lowered my head onto my bent knees and closed my eyes.

I hated that somebody would have to find me that way. It wasn't fair to them to find a human popsicle, and it would be traumatizing. Scaring someone for the rest of their life was certainly not my intention, but I just had no other options left.

3

HARRIS

I glanced into the rearview mirror and smiled. "Are you doing okay back there, girl?"

Luna lifted her head off her front paws and looked up at me before lying back down. She really was a sweetheart. Maybe she wasn't the brightest dog in the world, but she was already perfect for me. Apparently, as the runt of her litter, she got babied by her siblings. And the family who was training her wasn't very strict with her rules either. Which meant she needed a Daddy to give her guidance and structure and a purpose.

She gave me a purpose too.

But she definitely had a lot of quirks.

At least that was what the rescue lady told me. She didn't go into a lot of detail, but she told me not to be surprised if Luna randomly flopped her body on me or fetched a beer from the fridge without being asked. Neither of those seemed like much of a problem, so I wasn't worried.

What I had been more concerned about was a hyper puppy who needed to constantly run and play. But so far, she was pretty mellow. Even though she was only two, she seemed content to lie around and nap.

She and I were going to get along just fine.

The snow was coming down pretty hard as I crossed yet another state line. I'd been driving or sleeping in my car for the past twenty-four hours and couldn't wait to get home. If I didn't have to stop because of ice or a white-out, the GPS put me in my driveway by 4 AM. If we had to pull over and wait for the sun to rise, we'd be home closer to noon. Either way, we had food and water and blankets in the truck, so we'd be okay.

Speaking of food, I glanced back at Luna again. "Are you ready for a treat? You're being such a good girl."

Her ears perked up at the word treat, and she quickly stood on the backseat and dropped her head on my shoulder. But she didn't nudge me or gently tap my side.

No, the full weight of her big head landed square on my shoulder, and she pressed against the side of my face, reminding me she was there.

I chuckled and leaned against her. "Okay, okay. Give me a second to grab one." I reached into the bag of food and treats the lady gave me and pulled out a small milk bone for her. "Here you go. We'll be home soon."

She inhaled the bone in one breath and licked up the side of my cheek before planting herself across the backseat again.

That was the most action I'd gotten in a long time, so I didn't even wipe away her slobber. If she was a licker, I'd have to get used to it.

The radio played quietly, but I was enjoying the snowflakes that gently landed on the windshield before drifting away. Luna was going to love getting out and playing in the snow. I was told she'd fetch a ball, but I didn't know if she would run around by herself or if she would make me run with her.

That image brought a smile to my face. If I tried to run in the snow, I'd probably look like an abominable snowman.

I wasn't fat, but I definitely wasn't thin.

When I was in my twenties, I was pretty ripped. But as I moved through my thirties, the rivers and valleys of my abs turned into ponds and shorelines. And even though I worked out regularly, there was less definition than there used to be.

I still had the strength I'd had in my prime because of a mostly manual job, but without devoting hours to actual weight lifting, I had more of a "dad bod" than I liked to admit.

Fortunately, there were plenty of boys who were into dad bods like mine. I just hadn't found the right one yet.

When I saw a gas station up ahead, I pulled over to fuel up and take a piss. In case we did get stuck on the side of the road for a few hours, I wanted to make sure I could leave the engine running so we didn't freeze to death. At least, there wasn't much traffic on the road. The fewer idiots making bad decisions in the weather, the easier my life was.

The dark road was lined with widely spaced houses and woods on both sides. Most houses had many acres between them, so there was plenty of privacy for the people who lived there. It seemed peaceful in the dead of night.

I slowed down a bit, anxious to get home but aware that if something happened to the truck, we probably wouldn't have any cars passing by till morning. A rare streetlight flickered up ahead, and I realized it was shining over an enclosed bus stop. The plexiglass walls were scratched up and covered in graffiti, but with a quick glance, I recognized the shape of someone inside.

On instinct, my foot eased off the gas pedal, and I slowed down before finally flipping a U-turn and heading back to the bus stop. I couldn't imagine there were any buses running that late, and anybody sitting for a prolonged period of time out there would freeze to death.

I slowly passed the bus stop opening to make sure I wasn't imagining it, but there was definitely a body crumpled up on the bench.

"Fuck, is that a dead body?"

As if she could tell something was up, Luna stood on the backseat and her big head landed on my shoulder again.

"It's okay, Luna. We're just gonna go see who's out there."

I backed up so I was right in front of the opening to the bus shelter and rolled down my window, hoping the person would come to me.

When they didn't so much as stir, I started to get nervous. I cranked up the heat in the cab and hopped out of my truck to go check for myself.

A small wisp of a man was curled up in such a tight ball, I couldn't tell if he was breathing or not. Despite the thick jacket he wore, it was obvious he was freezing.

"Hey, there. You okay?" I kneeled down right in front of the man and tried to make eye contact.

His head was buried inside the crook of his elbow, so I couldn't see if he acknowledged me or not.

"Hey, man." I nudged his shoulder, gently at first and then with a little more force. "You can't stay here. You're gonna freeze to death."

He twitched just enough to let me know he was alive, but he didn't say a word as his head slowly lifted up and turned toward me. After a few seconds of him just staring, it seemed like his eyes were able to focus on me, and he swallowed hard. "I'm fine. Just leave me be."

Not today, kiddo. "Nope. We need to get you warmed up. Can you walk?"

His eyes fluttered shut, and he started to lean toward me as if he had lost consciousness. *Fuck.* I scooped him up in my arms and carried him into the front seat of the truck. I didn't know what else to do with him, but I couldn't just leave him there to die.

By the time I jogged around the front of my truck and got into the driver's seat, Luna had hopped over the center console and draped her whole body over this poor guy.

"Luna, backseat. You're gonna crush him."

The man shook his head slightly and wrapped both arms around her neck, probably soaking in her warmth.

"Oh, okay. Well, let me know if she gets too heavy."

He lowered his face onto the back of her neck and sucked in a deep breath before the tears started to flow down his cheek.

4

JESSE

Why does this keep happening? Why can't I just die and be done with it all?

I felt warm tears stream down my cheeks, but they were quickly replaced by an equally warm tongue, lapping at them. Where the hell did this dog come from? I had no idea what was going on, but I was pretty sure I was still alive, and as hot air blew across my body, reality came into sharper focus.

I could no longer pretend it was almost over.

"Why are you doing this? You should've just left me."

"Left you?" A man with a deep voice was very close to me, but I didn't dare open my eyes to look at him. If he was anything like Bruce, one wrong glance could end very painfully. "Why the hell were you out here in this weather? There aren't any buses coming this late."

"What time...?" I glanced at the dashboard and saw that it was just after midnight. How long had I been out there? Not long enough. "Oh."

"We need to get you to the hospital. You probably have hypothermia, and if you want to keep your fingers and toes, we need to get you warmed up."

I shook my head and reached for the door. "No, no hospital. I can't go to a hospital here. I'm fine."

A heavy hand landed over mine and stopped me before I could open the door.

Great. I had escaped one tyrant to be rescued by another. Sounds about right.

"You can't go back out there right now. You need to warm up first. Is there someone I can call? Somewhere I can take you?"

"No." I shook my head. "Just away."

His hand was still on mine for a moment before he gently lifted it off the handle and placed it back on the dog in my lap. "Away where?"

"As far as you're going. I just need to get away from here."

His fingers trailed up the side of my temple and brushed back some of the hair that was crusted with blood. After a thorough investigation of the visible injuries, his jaw clenched, and he inhaled deeply through his nose. "Where is he?"

I wanted to lie and tell the stranger I had just fallen and bumped my head, but my body wouldn't let me. I didn't have the strength to pretend anymore. Instead, I burst into full-body sobs, unable to stop myself from finally reacting to the past two years of hell I just escaped from. This guy might be my next captor, but I couldn't focus on anything other than being away from Bruce. It didn't matter how that happened. "As long as I can get out of this town, he won't find me."

The man's fingers gently traced along my face and down my arms until I winced at the pain in my elbow. "I'm only going to ask you this one more time. Where is he?"

I took in a deep breath in an attempt to control my crying and pointed my thumb over my shoulder. "He lives off Boone and Andal. A few miles back."

Before I could say anything else, he slammed on the brakes and flipped the truck around. On the icy road, the back of the truck bed fishtailed a bit, but he kept it between the lines and hit the gas.

"Please don't take me back. He'll kill me."

The man stared straight ahead with a determined look on his face. "No, he won't."

Goddammit. This was one of his friends. I didn't recognize him, but clearly he had been sent to find me and take me back. I considered reaching for the door handle again, but there was no way I could outrun this guy and his dog. I would be hard-pressed to even jump out with the weight of the dog pinning me to the seat.

I closed my eyes and accepted my fate. At least I tried. I was almost there. Wherever *there* was after death, I was close. But I had a feeling I'd get *there* soon enough.

We got to the main intersection, and he turned to me. "Left or right?"

"Don't you know?" If he knew Bruce, he should know where he lived.

"Left or right?"

"Left," I whispered. Maybe this was a test. So he could report back to Bruce whether or not I tried lying to him.

"How far up?"

Why the hell would Bruce send somebody out searching for me without giving him the address? "The driveway on the right. Just past those tires."

As soon as we got to the driveway, the man turned off the headlights on his truck and slowly rolled toward the trailer parked at the end of the lot. There were no additional lights turned on, so I wondered if Bruce was still asleep. But then... how could he still be asleep if he sent someone out to find me? Nothing was making sense, but I attributed that to my frozen brain. Maybe my body was shutting down and this was just a final survival push before I completely turned off.

He rolled to a stop at the end of the driveway, then reached underneath his seat and pulled out a revolver.

My eyes went wide, and I wondered if he thought I was going to try to run. "I'll go. You don't need that."

His face scrunched up in a confused expression, and then he shook his head once. "Wait in the truck."

My jaw hung open as this stranger got out of the truck and marched straight toward the front door of the trailer. Part of me considered jumping out and hiding in the trees so I could at least die in peace, but the truck was so warm, and when that man told me to wait, something in me wanted to obey him.

So, like the idiot I usually was, I just sat and stared as he stood at the front door for a few seconds before kicking it open.

5

HARRIS

What the hell am I doing?

Picking up a stranger on the side of the road during a bad storm was one thing. I was fine with being a decent human, but was I really going to shoot a stranger?

None of those questions were answered before I kicked open the door to the dilapidated doublewide, but when I took a quick glance around the room and saw empty bottles, lots of blood, and some piece of shit reaching for a 12 gauge, everything seemed to make perfect sense.

This was the fucker who had been abusing that kid. And he was scared for his life. The man was too young to be his father, which pissed me off even more because that probably meant he was some kind of a boyfriend. As the barrel of the shotgun slowly swung toward me, I lifted my revolver and put a bullet in his head.

It was all over pretty quickly, and the mess I left behind was much smaller than the one he'd created. I looked around to see if there was anything sentimental that the kid might want to take with him, but it all just looked like trash and other paraphernalia. I went back toward the bedroom area and saw a wallet. There wasn't much cash inside, but I pulled it out and slipped it into my pocket. The kid deserved a hell of a lot more than a few bucks, but that was all he'd be taking with him from the trailer, other than whatever broken bones and haunted memories had been also created there.

There was a half empty bottle of whisky on the table, so I dumped it onto the guy's lap and reached for one of the many lighters littered around the kitchen. With a single flame, his clothes were engrossed and whatever ghosts that were trapped in those walls were about to be permanently excised.

I stepped out of the trailer and looked around, half expecting to see blue and red lights flashing in the distance. But we were so far away from any neighbors, there was no way anybody could have heard the sound of gunfire or seen the flash of light. From where I was standing, I couldn't see into the truck, but I knew he was still there.

Probably scared to death, but hopefully also relieved.

I calmly marched back to the truck and slipped my gun into the holster attached underneath the seat before I hopped inside.

Luna was still covering most of his body with hers, and the boy's eyes were wide. "Is he really gone?"

I turned to him and nodded before backing the truck all the way up the driveway the way I came in. "Yep. You don't have to worry about him anymore. So, now, where can I take you?"

He sucked in a deep breath, and it looked like all the tension in his body rolled out of him on the exhale. "Any town is fine. I'll figure something out from there."

I pulled the small wad of cash from my pocket and handed it to him. "I think this is yours. But that's not enough to start over in a random town. Don't you have any family? Some friends you can stay with for a while?"

He turned away from me, facing the window. "There's no one, but I'll be fine. I just need to get away from here."

I didn't know the area well, but I knew there wasn't much industry for a few hundred miles, so I considered my options. I could get him a room in the closest hotel I came across and drop him off there. Or I could take him to one of the shelters in the city. There were more resources available there, and it would be easier for him to find a job.

But I knew I wasn't going to do either of those things. As stupid as it was, I let my Daddy side sneak out, and I decided I was going to take care of him. "You can stay at my place. I've got empty rooms, and I know some people who can give you a job."

He glanced at the money in his hand and scoffed. "I don't have money to pay you or anything. I'll be fine on my own."

I wanted to say something about how well that had been working out for him so far, but I didn't want to be a dick. "What's your name, anyway?"

"Jesse."

I turned and raised an eyebrow, waiting for more than that.

"Jesse Kramer."

"It's good to meet you, Jesse Kramer. I'm Harris Martins."

He nodded and looked straight out the window, probably as overwhelmed by the situation as I was. After several long and silent minutes, he cleared his throat and turned back to me. "Why did you do that? To Bruce, I mean. Don't get me wrong, I'm glad you did. But why didn't you just drop me off somewhere?"

That was the question of the hour. Why the fuck did I do that? "I don't like bullies. And even if you got away, he would always be looking for you. At least, that's what you'd believe, and you could never live in peace. Besides, there would be someone else he hurt after you." I shrugged as I ran out of words to describe what motivated me to end a stranger's life. "It's not something I go around doing every day, but I have no regrets about what just happened." I turned and looked him right in the eyes. "Do you?"

He shook his head, holding my gaze. "None."

"All right then. So, do you want to come home with me?"

He wrapped his arms around Luna again and chuckled. "Well, I don't think your dog would let me go anywhere else if I wanted to, so yeah, thank you."

6

JESSE

What is happening right now?

Bruce was a horrible human and the biggest asshole I'd ever met, but I didn't know for sure if he was a murderer. I thought he was close to becoming one...and had I stayed, he would have definitely been one sooner rather than later, but I didn't know that he actually was one.

Harris, on the other hand, definitely was. I basically watched him murder a total stranger.

For me.

What the fuck...

I should have been terrified and working out how I could get as far away from Harris as possible, but none of those instincts were firing inside me. The sense of relief outweighed any fear or self-preservation that should have been inside me.

Instead of worrying about what might happen next, I let my eyes drift shut and thought about the fact that I was still alive. Alive and warm.

I fell asleep quickly but kept waking up to images of Bruce—hovering over me, slamming the butt of his gun against my head, or kicking me before throwing a bottle in my direction.

Every time I jolted awake, the dog in my lap moaned her support and a heavy hand reached for my shoulder, gently reminding me that I was okay.

Those were words I hadn't thought in a very long time. *I'm okay.*

Nothing about my situation should have felt okay, but that was all I could come up with when I glanced at Harris and saw the lights of the city finally coming into view.

"You drove all night." The sun was just starting to rise, and he didn't look the least bit tired. "Don't you need to sleep?"

"I'm fine. How about you? You must be hungry."

My stomach rumbled, and Luna's ears perked up. She must be ready for breakfast too. "I'm okay."

Harris looked straight ahead, but I could see his eye twitch before he inhaled deeply and turned to me. "I know you don't have any reason to trust me yet, but I would appreciate it if you don't lie to me. If you're hungry, don't say you're not. If you're in pain, don't tell me you're fine." He glanced at the road then back at me, holding my gaze. "Can you do that?"

"Yeah." I swallowed hard as I nodded. "I guess I could eat."

"Good. Me too. I want to get you to the clinic to make sure nothing's broken or frostbitten, and then we'll go grab breakfast."

I looked down at my filthy jacket, knowing the shirt underneath was torn and bloodied. "I'm not really dressed to go anywhere. Can we do all that later...or tomorrow?" Or never. Preferably never.

"No, Jesse. I have a friend who's a doctor. He won't ask you any more questions than necessary, and I trust him to be discreet. I just don't want to be responsible for you not getting the treatment you need because you're embarrassed about something you shouldn't be."

I wanted to argue, but there really was a lot of blood crusted on my jeans and shoes. It seemed likely there might be more damage than I thought. "I don't have insurance. How much will it cost?"

Harris placed his hand on Luna's back, just inches away from where mine was resting. "He's not gonna charge you for an exam. Don't worry about that. Let's just get you back to one piece and we'll figure things out from there."

"Okay," I whispered. What was there to figure out? All I really needed was an address I could use for a job application and a place to shower now and then so I could be presentable. Why was he taking such a strong interest in my health...unless he was just worried I might tell someone what he did? "And...I won't tell anyone what happened. Ever. I promise."

His gaze caught mine again, and he gave me a small smile. "I know, Jesse."

As much as I wanted to believe that Harris just had some kind of hero complex and would do all this for any random stranger, deep in my gut, I wondered if maybe there was something more to his kindness.

He was hot as hell, with a short beard and muscles that filled out his flannel shirt and coat deliciously. I'd always had a thing for older guys, and with his dark hair and eyes that could practically see right through me, I couldn't help but imagine him wanting to do more than just nurse me back to health.

Then again, I almost felt the same way about Bruce in the beginning. Almost. At first, I thought Bruce was kind of cute. He didn't give off the sexy Daddy vibe like Harris, but he was good-looking enough that I wasn't immediately afraid of him. When he offered me a place to stay, I believed he was just a good guy, too. That lasted all of about two nights. And then things went from bad to worse.

When he was sober, he would apologize and tell me he loved me and he'd beg me to stay. And as stupid as it sounded, I always did.

I couldn't be that gullible ever again.

I wouldn't survive it.

But Harris was different. I did have something to hold over his head, so if he treated me badly, I could go to the police. I knew I wouldn't, but I could. So, as long as Harris was being kind, I didn't really have much choice other than to accept his generosity and hope for the best.

Besides, anybody with a dog this sweet had to be a decent human.

As if she could sense me staring down at her, Luna stood up, circled her giant body around my lap, and then flopped back down in a ginormous lump. "She obviously thinks she's a lapdog."

Harrris chuckled. "Yeah, she's not the brightest dog ever, but she sure seems to like you."

I leaned forward so she could lick my face. "Bright or not, at least she's warm."

7

HARRIS

"Tony, wake up."

One of my best friends was a great general practitioner, but he wasn't a morning person. "Hmm..."

He picked up the phone but clearly wasn't fully awake because I immediately heard heavy breathing on the line, like he was already asleep again. "Tony!"

"Yeah, I'm up." He yawned loudly and cleared his throat. "Harris?"

"Yeah, sorry to call so early, but I need you to see someone for me. Can we meet at your clinic?"

"Now?" There was a scratching sound from his end, and he inhaled deeply. "What's going on? Are you okay?"

At least he was awake now. "I'm fine, but a friend of mine might need some stitches. And he was caught in the storm last night. Can you just do a quick exam to make sure all his fingers and toes look good?"

He was quiet for a moment, probably choosing his next words carefully. "Of course. I just need a few minutes to get dressed, and then I'll meet you down there. How far out are you?"

"About ten minutes." Tony lived in a condo above his clinic. Well, twelve stories above his clinic. It was a large building with retail and office space on the first floor. A convenient set-up for his small practice and great for emergency situations like this. "Thanks, man."

"The door will be open, so just come on in when you get here."

I'd barely hit the End button on my phone when Jesse started to freak out. "Are you sure this is a good idea? What am I supposed to say? He's gonna think I'm suicidal for being out in that weather. He could commit me for a psychiatric hold or something."

I placed my hand on his forearm, choosing a spot that seemed to have minimal damage. When he didn't flinch, I gave him a gentle squeeze. "He isn't going to commit you. I promise." I pulled my hand away and rested it on Luna's flank. "Were you? Suicidal, I mean."

His eyes got glossy, and he shrugged. "Not really. I left because I didn't want Bruce to kill me. But I guess I did consider the fact that I might not survive the weather. But now, I'm not. Promise."

"I believe you." At least, I wanted to. "Tony's a good guy. He'll take care of you."

"Okay." His voice was still soft, but he wasn't quite as terrified as he seemed earlier. "If you say so."

He trusted me.

An unexpected wave of...something...washed through me. I couldn't name it because I couldn't remember ever feeling it before, but I knew it was a good thing. At least, I hoped it was.

Without any other discussion, I parked in front of Tony's clinic and killed the engine. "We're here."

Luna lifted her head, probably as eager as we were to get out of the truck. "Sorry, girl. You've got a few more minutes in here. Then we'll walk, okay?"

She moaned and shifted her weight so Jesse could slip out from underneath her and exit the truck.

"We'll be quick." I gave her another treat before locking up the truck and heading inside.

Tony was standing at the door, holding it open as we approached. He took a look at Jesse from head to toe then raised an eyebrow at me.

"You should see the other guy." I grinned at Tony and winked at Jesse when he turned to me with a slack jaw.

"I don't think I want to..." Tony held out his hand toward the first exam room. "Right this way and we'll get you checked out."

He looked at me and then Jesse. "Um, how about we have Harris wait out here?"

I bristled at the suggestion but kept my features neutral so he wouldn't feel pressured either way.

Jesse looked at me then back at Tony. "Yeah, okay."

Damn. I was hoping he'd want me to go in with him. "I'll walk Luna around the block and be right back. Call if you need me." I was looking at Jesse as I spoke, but I was also letting Tony know I'd only be a few minutes, and I expected a full report when I returned.

"We'll be fine." Tony glanced over my shoulder to the truck outside. "Is Luna your dog? Bring her in when you get back. She can wait in here." He nodded to the waiting area.

"Okay, thanks." I wanted to stay and hear all the details, but I didn't have that right. Not yet. Maybe not ever. That thought made my stomach tighten. "I'll be back in a minute."

Begrudgingly, I left the office and went back to the truck. Luna was waiting for me with her slobbery face pressed to the window. I guess she was ready for breakfast.

I tapped the window and pointed at her to back up so I could open the door without her tumbling out. Her tail started to wag as soon as she saw me reach for her food and water bowls before filling them both up and placing them on the sidewalk. "Okay, girl. Let's eat up so we can go potty."

She hopped down and quickly finished her food before lapping up half the water in her bowl. I glanced inside to see if Tony or Jesse were there, but the lobby was empty. So, I put the leash on Luna, and we headed toward a park on the other side of the block.

We weren't gone for more than fifteen minutes, but I was disappointed to find the lobby still empty when Luna and I went inside. I wanted to peek into the exam room to make sure everything was okay, but I knew that would be overstepping. Jesse had a right to privacy, and I was sure he'd tell me whatever diagnosis Tony shared with him.

I paced back and forth in front of the reception desk before the exam room door opened, and Tony poked his head out. "You want to come in here for a minute?"

"Um, sure. If that's okay with Jesse." I was already in the room, not waiting for an answer from either of them. "How's our patient?"

Jesse smiled and held up his left arm, which was encased in a soft cast. "Just a hairline fracture."

"Not *just* a hairline fracture. Any fracture is serious, and this could easily become a full break if you aren't careful with it." Tony waited for Jesse to acknowledge what he'd said before turning to me. "I closed a few lacerations with dissolvable stitches, so he doesn't need those removed, but I do want to check on his arm in four weeks if there isn't any pain or additional trauma."

"There won't be." I directed my stare to Jesse and his breath caught. "Everything else is okay?"

Tony glanced at the notes on his tablet and shrugged. "Lots of bruises, both new and old, but no tissue damage from the cold, so he should be good as new with some rest and a warm meal."

Jesse's stomach rumbled again, and his cheeks turned pink. "Yeah, I guess I am kinda hungry."

I beamed with pride at him for being honest with me and Tony. "If we're done here, we can hit Martha's. Luna is all set, so she's probably napping again."

Tony handed me a few sheets of paper. "I gave him a couple Motrin and a prescription for something stronger. It might make him groggy or nauseous, so let me know if he needs anything else."

I gave my friend a half hug for his help. "Thanks, man. I owe you big time."

He grinned. "Don't worry about it. I'm keeping track and plan to cash in big someday."

As we were walking out, Jesse rushed forward to grab Luna's leash, and Tony pulled me back for a second. "So, do I want to ask what's going on with you two?"

"I don't know that anything is, but I couldn't not help him when I came across him last night." I sighed and looked at the broken boy hugging my dog. "For now, I'm just focused on getting him healthy. Besides, every good dog needs a boy, right?"

Tony chuckled and patted me on the back. "Yeah, he seems like a good boy. Just make sure you know what you're doing before making him *your* good boy."

Easier said than done.

8

JESSE

The pain meds I took at the clinic made me drowsy, so we picked up breakfast burritos, and then Harris took me back to his house. I don't know what I was expecting to find, but the well-manicured row house in the middle of Bucktown was not it.

When we pulled up in front of it, I was shocked. "Wow, this is your place?"

"Yeah." He put the truck in park and killed the engine. "Got it a few years ago at auction and have been fixing it up ever since."

"It's really nice." I'd always lived in shitty apartments or trailers, so what he probably considered to be a modest home looked like a damn mansion to me, but I tried to keep my cool as we walked up to the porch. "You've done a good job with it."

Harris shrugged and mumbled his thanks before unlocking the front door and waving me and Luna inside.

The inside was tidy with comfortable-looking furniture and just the right amount of stuff to make it look lived in. There were no empty beer bottles or pizza boxes strewn around, and the leather sofa was worn in all the right places. It was the perfect home. "Do you live here alone?"

"Yep. You're my first guest. So..." He pulled a treat out of the bag for Luna and then looked around the room. "Kitchen is straight ahead. To the left is a bathroom and the staircase, obviously." He grinned. "To the right is the official guest bedroom. It should be pretty comfortable, but I've never actually slept on that bed, so let me know if it's hard or lumpy or whatever."

"I'm sure it'll be fine. Thank you." I wasn't picky. I'd slept in some pretty shitty places, so his guest room would be like the Taj Mahal to me.

"My room, another bathroom, and the other spare room-slash-office is at the top of the stairs. Feel free to make yourself comfortable. Take a nap, take a shower, watch

TV. I'm gonna take Luna out back to do her business and then probably head upstairs to get a few hours of sleep myself."

"Oh, okay." I really didn't know what to do with myself, and I felt weird just wandering around in his house while he slept. "I can mostly just stay in the room."

He looked at me like I was crazy and shook his head. "No. If you're gonna stay here, consider this your home too." He held up a finger as he seemed to remember something. "Actually, one sec."

I watched him as he moved with a confidence and strength I didn't often see in men like him. He seemed like a regular guy who drove a regular truck and had a regular dog...but then he seemed like so much more than that too.

Like everything about him was...better.

He went to the kitchen and opened a drawer, then pulled out a key ring. "This is a key to the front and back door. Feel free to come and go as you please. Just make sure Luna is inside and lock the doors when you go out." He looked around again, as if making sure he'd covered all the basics. "Is there anything else you need right now?"

I reached for the key and winced. "No, I think I'm going to shower and nap too."

He winced too as if he could feel my pain or felt guilt for momentarily forgetting about it. "I've got some codeine from when I had a wisdom tooth pulled. I'll get that for you, and then we'll pick up the rest of the stuff Tony suggested later this afternoon."

He turned to walk toward the back of the house with Luna, seeming to trust me in his home, as if I were a life-long friend.

I just stood there, still in a bit of shock over what was happening. "Harris," I called out to him.

He stopped at the door and held it open for Luna to run outside. "Yes."

I held his gaze, almost breathless from the intensity of it. "Thank you. You have no idea how much this means to me."

He just nodded and then followed the dog outside.

———

The bed was like floating on a cloud.

My body still ached, and there was a dull throbbing in my head, but it was easy to ignore it all because I'd never been so comfortable in my life. I was wearing an old sweatshirt and my boxers, but the heavy down comforter held in enough heat to make me consider poking a few toes out from beneath it.

But I didn't do it. There wasn't any permanent frostbite damage, but I did have a few blisters that I needed to be careful with. Eventually, I opened my eyes and stretched my arms above my head.

Everything hurt.

As if placed there by an angel, a bottle of water and two high-dosage codeine tablets were on the nightstand.

I leaned over to grab the bottle and realized why the bed was so warm. Luna was pressed against my back, heating me like a warming pad. When I started to stir, she lifted her butt into the air and stretched her front legs like a cat before hopping off the bed.

Within seconds, Harris appeared, leaning against the door jamb. "How you feeling?"

"Better." I yawned and sat up. "Sore, but warm and rested."

"Good." He held up a mug. "Can I get you some coffee or tea?"

"Coffee sounds good." I glanced around the room, looking at the clock. "Is it really four in the afternoon?"

He grinned. "Don't feel bad. I just woke up about an hour ago myself...and I hardly ever sleep."

9

HARRIS

I shouldn't have been watching Jesse sleep. And it definitely shouldn't have been so arousing. But when he wasn't aware that I was looking and I could just stare, it was hard to imagine how he could get messed up with someone as dangerous as his ex. Then again, the fact that he was sleeping in my house, a stranger who had already murdered a man in cold blood, might have been an indicator that he didn't have a strong sense of self-preservation.

He looked so peaceful with his hands tucked under his face and the freckles on his cheeks barely visible in the dimly lit room. It was strangely sexy.

There was just something so innocent about him, even though he was clearly not a virgin. In fact, he probably had more past partners than I did.

Ugh. That thought didn't sit well in my gut.

But past partners were irrelevant.

I had a very specific kink, and most men did not fit it. The odds of Jesse being interested in what I needed were pretty slim, and none of that even mattered at the moment. What did matter was that he healed up without an infection and was finally safe from whatever demons had been chasing him.

And with just a few hours of rest, he looked a thousand times better.

I filled a mug with coffee and added a scoop of cocoa and some creamer to cut the bitterness. That late in the afternoon, he didn't need the extra caffeine, but he deserved something sweet after everything he'd just survived. Before leaving the kitchen, I filled another mug with the chicken noodle soup I'd warmed up from a can. Tony said he might not have much of an appetite for a while, but I wanted to keep Jesse nourished as much as possible.

In fact, without the ability to do much else for him, making sure he kept up his strength and didn't get weak or lightheaded was my singular focus. I was able to coax him into taking a few bites at breakfast before the painkillers started to really set in, but once they did, he could barely keep his eyes open.

When he'd dozed off on the drive, I imagined carrying him inside and taking him straight to bed.

But I couldn't be thinking that way. I was basically a stranger who'd picked him up off the side of the road. I had no right to offer anything more than food, shelter, and safety until he was on his feet.

I brought the tray from the kitchen into Jesse's room, and he was sitting up on the bed. Luna was sprawled across his lap, pinning him to the mattress. "You can tell her to move."

Jesse smiled and shrugged. "I've never had a dog. It's kinda nice."

"Well, she's gonna have to scoot over a bit for you to eat." I snapped my finger and pointed to the foot of the bed. "Luna, scootch."

She hopped up and off the bed, disappearing out of the room.

"Aww, you hurt her feelings." Jesse smiled. "She's probably gonna go pee in your shoes."

"She better not." I waited for him to situate himself against the headboard before placing the tray on his lap. "I have cocoa coffee and soup. But I can order in anything you want, if you'd prefer."

"Wow, thank you." His eyes went wide as he looked at the modest spread. "This is so...nice."

A warmth spread in my chest, but I kept my expression stoic. "It was nothing. Just following the doctor's orders."

He glanced at me from under long lashes, making the warmth spread southerly. "It wasn't nothing. You've been...everything. And I really appreciate it."

I'd never been good at accepting gratitude, so I cleared my throat and took a step back. "Don't mention it. I'll just—" Before I could finish my sentence, Luna jumped back on the bed and dropped a tape dispenser onto Jesse's hand.

"Um, thanks, Luna." He picked up the tape and looked at me. "Scotch tape?"

It took me a second to connect the dots before I barked out a laugh. "I was warned she might do this."

"Bring you tape?" He handed it to me and then nuzzled Luna's head against his neck. "Good girl, Luna. Thanks for the gift."

"I told her to scootch, and she must have thought I asked for Scotch. It's the reason she flunked out of service dog school. She has...selective hearing."

Jesse laughed when Luna grabbed the tape with a soft mouth and lobbed it at me. "You're gonna have to be careful what you say around her."

I picked up the tape and slipped it into my back pocket. "I'm just glad she went for tape instead of hitting up my bar. I've got a six-hundred-dollar bottle of Johnny Walker in there."

"Really?" Jesse's eyes went big as he took a sip of the coffee. "Mmm, this is good."

"Glad you like it." I wanted to hang out and chat with him, but I also wanted to give him space. He'd been through a lot with a violent and aggressive man. I didn't want him to think I was overbearing or hovering when I was just trying to take care of him. "I should leave you to eat your lunch in peace. If you need anything, I'll just be out here in the family room."

"Oh, okay." He bit the inside of his lip like he had some-thing else to say but then looked down at the dog. "Is it okay if Luna stays?"

"Of course." I patted his foot through the comforter then realized it might still be hurting. "Oh, shit. Sorry. Did that hurt?"

He smiled up at me but his mouth went lax when our gazes locked. "Not at all."

I didn't know what to say, afraid that whatever came out of my mouth would be completely inappropriate. So I just walked right out of the room.

We had plenty of time to get to know each other better. It hadn't even been twenty-four hours yet, and I'd already killed a man for him. Slowing things down seemed like the right move.

10

JESSE

Over the next few days, the pain in my body got worse. Breathing hurt, and every time I lifted my arm, I had to hold in a cry. But the surprising part was the way that Harris doted on me, appearing at my side with water or painkillers or a snack at every turn.

I'd never felt so...cared for. My mom wasn't meant to be a mom, and the men that were shuffled in and out of our lives were not good men.

I think that's probably why I'd always gravitated toward assholes. The kind of guys who treated me like shit and made me believe I was lucky to have them. But Harris wasn't like that. Not at all. He didn't seem burdened or annoyed by the fact that I needed so much help to do everything.

In fact, it seemed like he enjoyed it. Thrived on it.

When Harris finally went back to work a few days later, he checked on me throughout the day and still managed to take care of me. Not just by making sure I took my meds and stretched my legs on a regular basis, but the man was obsessed with food. He brought breakfast to me before he left in the mornings, came back with lunch at exactly twelve-fifteen in the afternoon, and then he brought dinner home from local restaurants every night.

I'd never been one to eat three full meals every day, so it was a little much at first, but I quickly got used to the attention and was even putting on a few pounds, something I hadn't done since high school.

After about a week, I was able to move around better. My soft cast was off more often than it was on, but I wanted to start using it as soon as possible so I wouldn't lose too much muscle tone. I didn't have a ton, but keeping my arm functional was important to me.

I left the bedroom and started watching TV in the family room so I could hang out with Harris. He was surprised at first but welcomed me to join him on the couch beside Luna.

As soon as I sat down, she stood up, made a few circles on the cushion between us, and then plopped down against my side.

"Oof." I flinched at the weight of her landing on me but appreciated her attention. "Has she gained weight?"

"Probably." Harris reached around and placed his hand under her flank to shift her weight. "Back off him, girl. You're too heavy."

"She's fine." I placed my hand on his, and he went stock still, his gaze locking with mine as all the air in the room seemed to evaporate around us.

Neither of us moved for several long moments while the heat of his rough skin penetrated my fingers, warming me up. He'd touched me a hundred times, but this time felt different. Like it was more than just a clinical examination or a friend helping change the bandages of someone else.

The heat in his eyes was unmistakable.

And the tenting in my sweats was too. Before I embarrassed myself any further, I removed my hand and shook off the intensity of the touch. He was just being his usual kind self, and I was taking advantage of that.

If I wanted to stay with him, and I really did, I needed to control myself. "Sorry about that."

"Don't be." He continued to look right at me before clearing his throat. "Anyway, I was just gonna start a movie. You want me to make some popcorn?"

I smiled and carded my fingers through Luna's soft coat. "Yeah, that sounds good."

"Great." Harris jumped off the sofa and headed toward the kitchen. "I even have a bag of M&Ms from the last time I went to the movies. Want me to throw those in too?"

"M&Ms in popcorn?" I'd never heard of such a thing. "Won't they melt?"

He looked at me over his shoulder and winked. "That's the best part. A few will open up and make a mess, but the majority of them will stay whole and explode in your mouth when you bite down on them."

A shiver ran down my spine at that visual...not of the candy-coated chocolates but of an explosion in my mouth of an entirely different kind. "Um, yeah. That sounds perfect."

I grabbed a throw blanket from the back of the sofa and covered my lap, just in case the movie got sexy. Or more likely, in case my eyes drifted from the screen and landed on the sexy man who had been treating me like royalty, nursing me back to health, and showering me with attention since the moment we met.

I was strategically positioned on one end of the sofa when Harris returned with a bowl and two cans of Coke. Luna had her head on my lap, and her body was stretched out across the other two cushions when Harris handed me a can.

"Seriously, dog." He sighed and then lifted her back half up high enough that he could slip beneath her. "Must you claim every inch that we want to be in?"

There was nothing inappropriate about what he said, but I couldn't help grinning at the innuendo. Harris caught my smile and smirked. "You'd think she was trained to be a weighted blanket."

I tilted my body so I was angled in Harris's direction. "I've always wanted one of those heavy blankets. I think she's an excellent alternative."

He wedged the large bowl between the back cushion and Luna's elbow. "Well, she makes a good table, if nothing else."

Harris hit the play button on the remote and The King began to play. The guys on the screen were all pretty hot, but my attention kept wandering over to the much hotter man beside me.

Now and then, our fingers would brush against each other when we were grabbing chocolatey popcorn at the same time. And every time it happened, my breath would catch and I'd freeze in place, wondering if he'd be mad or glad or...anything.

But his stoic expression didn't break.

It was so hard to read him. Sometimes, I could practically feel the lust and desire in the air when Harris was helping with my bandages or brushing stray hair from my forehead. But other times, moments like this, I had no idea what he was thinking.

Did he have the same impure thoughts about me that I had about him? If I made a move, would he be open to it or disgusted? He knew my secrets and had seen me at my absolutely lowest moment in life. Why would a man like him stoop so low as to be interested in me romantically?

There was no way it would happen.

But that didn't stop me from wanting it. Imagining him pulling me into his arms as more than a caring friend but as a lover. A man who wanted to take care of all my needs...not just the medical ones.

The movie was two hours long, and about halfway through, my eyelids grew heavy. I tried to stay awake, but I kept dozing off, so I lay down with my head on the armrest and my legs curled up in a tight ball. Luna groaned and stood up, stepping around me as she tried to find a new comfortable position.

To my shock and surprise, Harris grabbed my socked feet and placed them on his lap so Luna could sprawl on the cushion in front of me, locking me against the back of the sofa.

I wanted to say something, thank him or otherwise acknowledge his gesture, but no words came. I just closed my eyes and enjoyed the way his big hands softly rubbed the balls of my feet, warming them up and lulling me into a deep slumber.

11

HARRIS

By the time the credits were rolling, Jesse was fast asleep.

His soft breaths were barely audible, but his whole chest moved with each inhale. For several minutes, I just sat there and watched him. Somehow, throughout the movie, my hand ended up rubbing his socked foot. I wasn't sure if he even noticed, but just having that small connection to him made me want more.

I briefly considered leaving him on the couch with Luna and a few blankets to keep warm, but I was afraid he'd wake up in even more pain. I'd fallen asleep on that couch a few times and always regretted it the next day. So, after carefully standing up, I slid my arms underneath him— one right under his ribs while the other hooked below his thighs—and lifted him up.

Jesse began to stir, but instead of resisting, his face nestled underneath my chin, and he seemed to curl into me.

I wondered if he had woken up when his palm flattened against my chest and then closed around the fabric of my cotton shirt, but his breathing was slow and even, confirming that the movements were merely instinct and not a reflection of his interest in me.

Moving as smoothly as possible, I took him into his room and managed to pull back the covers so I could lay him between the sheets without jarring him too much.

"Mmm, that's nice." His whispered words startled me, but when I looked at his face, his eyes were closed and he was still asleep.

Apparently, he was a sleep talker.

Before stepping away, I brushed a few loose strands of hair across his forehead and trailed my thumb down to his jaw. He was so beautiful. Such a perfect, sweet boy.

The expression on his face changed, and I worried I had woken him, but his hips jutted forward, and he moaned softly with a dreamy look.

Oh, shit. This boy was having a sex dream.

My cock was instantly interested in learning more about Jesse's nighttime fantasies, but I felt like a creeper just standing over him as he slept. He deserved privacy, and I had to give it to him, even when I didn't want to.

It wasn't easy, but after a few more throaty sounds that definitely seemed to be indicative of a happy ending to his dream, I turned on my heel and left his room.

Besides, I suddenly had my own nighttime fantasies to work through.

After getting everything put away downstairs, I took Luna out back one last time and then headed up to my room. She took about two steps up the stairs before turning around and heading back to sleep with Jesse. Traitor.

She hadn't slept with me once since I brought her home.

Knowing he was out for the night, I got undressed and slipped into my bed completely naked. My cock was already semi-hard, but as soon as I started thinking about the sounds and movements Jesse was making in his sleep, it became a solid rod that I couldn't ignore.

At first, I loosely teased the head, tapping the glans around the outside and tip before fully stroking from the top to the base. It was still early, and I didn't have to work in the morning, so I took my time, imagining what Jesse would look like in my bed.

Every time I got to the point of almost coming, I'd release my dick and let the moment pass, edging for a long while before finally being ready to give in. With the sound of his soft moaning still ringing in my ears, I began to stroke faster, no longer fighting the ache in my balls to finally release. With Jesse's sweet face and trusting eyes vividly staring at me in my mind, I came abruptly, shaking hard and spewing load after load of thick cream onto my hand and belly.

Fuck, I needed that.

Too lazy to get up, I lay there for a moment, gently sliding my fingers across my slick belly as the tremors finally subsided.

Just as I made the decision to get cleaned up, Luna started barking from downstairs.

I'd never really heard her bark, so I was immediately nervous.

Without thinking, I hopped out of my bed and ran down the stairs, entering Jesse's bedroom with enough adrenaline to eliminate any threat that was posed against him.

Luna stood over him, licking his face as he whimpered on the bed, still fully asleep.

I immediately went to his other side to wake him up. "Jesse, baby. Wake up."

"Noooo…" He flailed on the mattress, crying out in terror. "Please don't hurt me."

My hands closed around his slight wrists to hold him in place and keep him from hurting himself or Luna. "Jesse, it's me. Harris. No one is going to hurt you. Ever." I shook him harder when his eyes still didn't open. "Wake up, baby."

Luna started barking again, and that seemed to finally break through to him.

Jesse's eyes flew open, and he pulled back from me, pressing his back against the headboard as he adjusted to his environment. "Harris?"

Luna stepped over his lap and dropped right onto him, holding him in place as he tried to catch his breath.

"Yeah, it's me. You were having a nightmare." He and I both seemed to realize at the same moment that I was still completely naked, so I reached for a pillow and covered myself with it. "Sorry, I was in bed when I heard Luna barking. I didn't stop to get dressed."

He pulled the sheet up to his chest, wadding up the fabric between his fists. "I'm sorry for waking you. It was just so...real."

"What were you dreaming? Unless you don't want to talk about it." I had a pretty good idea, but if he wanted to talk about it, I would be there to listen to him. "It might help you go back to sleep."

He took a deep breath, and his shoulders relaxed. "Well, you were there..."

My jaw dropped as I thought about the fear in his voice. "I was hurting you?"

"No," he said quickly. "That wasn't you. The dream started out...good. I was here. And you were too. Anyway, in my dream, we went to sleep, and then... Bruce was there, and he had a gun."

I placed my hand around the side of his neck and ran my thumb along the smooth skin. "He's gone, Jesse. He'll never hurt you again. I promise."

"I know, but..." Jesse looked at me for a moment and then focused his gaze down on Luna. "In my dream, he hurt you first."

"Me?" I ran back the details of his story in my head, trying to piece together the full picture. "Did you walk into my room while he was hurting me?"

Jesse shook his head but still didn't meet my gaze. "I was already in there when he came."

Fuck. That was exactly what I wanted to hear, but also the last thing I needed to be thinking about in that moment. I gave his neck a gentle squeeze before letting my palm trail down his shoulder to his fisted hands. I pulled them forward and clasped his hands between mine. "Any time you have thoughts about him, I want you to remind yourself that he's gone. He will never hurt you again. Whether you're awake or asleep, whether I'm with you or not, he can never get near you again."

Jesse finally locked his eyes on mine and nodded. "I know. Thank you."

Some wet hair clung to the side of his face in chunks, and I could see sweat still glistening from his temples. "Do you feel like you could go back to sleep or would you like to watch some TV? Maybe take a shower."

His eyes darted back to Luna as he softly whispered, "I think I need a shower."

"Okay, can I help you with anything?" I stood up, still holding the pillow in front of my lap. "Actually, maybe I should go get dressed first."

Jesse glanced and the pillow then up at me. "Unless you wanna shower too."

My heart slowed down and every beat thudded through my body. "Would you like some help?"

His breath hitched, and he nodded. "Yes, please."

Fuck, this boy is messing with fire.

12

JESSE

I couldn't believe I just said that. What was I thinking? Did he think I was a pervert?

Harris just stood there for a couple very long seconds before he tossed the pillow onto the bed and reached out a hand for me. "Well, let's go then."

A shiver ran through me as I glanced down at his thick cock. I didn't know they could be so wide. There was no way something like that could fit inside me, but just the thought made my own dick start to twitch.

And that was when I realized something was wrong.

At first, I panicked, reaching down to feel if I'd wet the bed. But when my fingers landed in a puddle of cream on my thigh, I knew I didn't piss myself. My eyes were wide as I looked up at Harris. "Um, I think I need a minute."

"Why?" He looked at my eyes and then down to where my hand stopped in my lap. "What's wrong?"

I dropped my chin to my chest, mortified that he might learn my secret. "Please don't make me say it out loud."

He dropped to a crouch beside the bed and implored me with his eyes. "I won't make you do anything, but my nerves are frayed as hell at the moment, and knowing something is wrong that you won't tell me about is going to freak me out. So, please know that you can tell me anything. Good or bad, even if it's something I'm doing wrong, you can talk to me."

I didn't want to tell him, but I didn't want him to think it was about him. Technically, it was about him, but not in the way he was worrying about. I swallowed hard and squeezed my eyes shut. "I think I had...an accident. When I was asleep."

"Oh." His demeanor fully changed, and he went from being afraid of my response to almost relieved by it. "That's okay, Jess. Nothing to be ashamed of. Accidents happen all the time. Let's get you into the shower, and I'll change the sheets. It's no problem."

I tucked my hand underneath my thighs and ass and felt the mattress. Nope. Just as I suspected, the only issue was in my underwear and the front of my flannel pajama bottoms. "Actually, I think the sheets are fine. It was just...in my lap." I wanted to die, but I kept speaking until it was all out there. "I just need to change my clothes, but...it's still really embarrassing."

Harris's warm hand cupped my cheek, and his thumb slid across the top of my cheekbone until I opened my eyes and looked at him. "You have nothing to be embarrassed about. Truthfully, I would much rather hear about you having happy dreams every single night than ever think of you having nightmares. Please, don't feel bad. I'll go get the water running for the shower, and when you're ready, head in there."

I nodded against his warm palm. "Thank you."

Harris left the room, and Luna followed. I tried not to watch the way his ass moved from side to side as he went, but I couldn't help it. His wide frame held thick muscles, even though they were padded by a layer of skin and were only visible when he flexed them.

Once he was gone, I got out of the bed and slipped out of my pants and boxers. I didn't want to put fresh boxers on my sticky skin, so I grabbed a clean pair and pulled my sweatshirt down in the front to cover my dick.

I'd already seen Harris fully naked, and he'd caught glimpses of me in various states of undress during the week I'd been staying with him. If he was in fact going to help me in the shower, there was no sense in getting dressed for the short walk to the bathroom.

When I entered the guest bathroom, Harris had a towel wrapped around his waist, and hot water was steaming up the room. He was leaning inside the shower stall, adjusting the temperature. "I turned it on full blast, but it might be too hot now."

He turned to me just as I pulled my sweatshirt over my face to yank it off. His breath hitched as I stood there just as naked as he was under that towel.

"I like it hot." I stepped under the spray and let the scalding water hit my head and flow down my shoulders. It was a bit hotter than I usually liked it, but the sting was welcome.

It reminded me that I was still alive...and Bruce wasn't. That I would carry on and could finally be safe and happy. With Harris.

I turned beneath the water and looked for him. He was still standing on the mat beside the shower pan, watching me carefully. When my eyes locked on his, he knew what I needed without me having to say a word. He knew what I wanted before I could form a plan in my mind.

With the flick of his wrist, he released his towel and stepped into the shower with me.

My breath was frozen in my lungs as I waited for his next move. His first move.

Harris reached around my shoulder and grabbed a washcloth and bottle of body wash. Holding them both in front of me, he asked, "May I?"

I nodded, incapable of speaking and ruining the magical moment as he squeezed a dollop of soap on the towel and held it under the water to lather.

"The first part of your dream." He wadded up the towel in his hand and then placed it on my chest. "The good part of it." He gently rubbed up to one shoulder and then around my sternum to the other shoulder before placing his wet hand over one of my nipples. "Is that the part that I was in?"

I swallowed hard, overwhelmed by how good his skin felt on mine and how much I liked the way he looked at me. Like I was precious to him. "Yes, you made that happen...in my dream."

The towel slowly trailed down my stomach but stopped at my hairline, not venturing to the place I desperately wanted him to touch. "Would you like that to happen again? In real life?"

My head was spinning, and I wasn't sure I'd stay upright. Subtly shifting my weight, I leaned against the cool tile. "Yes."

Harris's pupils darkened as he stepped closer to me, sliding his soapy hand down between us. His firm grip closed around my cock, and he gently tugged, testing my responsiveness as I shivered under his touch. "I've wanted to feel you like this since the first time I saw you look at me..." His free hand lifted my chin until I was looking into his eyes. "Like this. Like I was your damn hero, and you'd follow me to the ends of the earth."

I licked my lips, even though they were wet from the spray bouncing between us. "I think I would...because you are."

Harris leaned forward, brushing his lips against mine as he began to stroke my cock, coaxing an orgasm out of me almost instantly. I wanted to apologize for my reaction but his thick dick twitched against my thigh, and I knew he wasn't mad at me.

He was proud.

"God, Harris, that—"

He kissed me harder, stopping my words by slipping his tongue into my mouth as he used my come to lubricate his own cock against my hips. "Not my name. Not when we're like this. When we're like this, you're my boy, and I'm your Daddy. Is that okay with you?"

He gave me an option that I wanted to take. He wasn't forcing me, but rather inviting me to be his. I whimpered in his arms, grateful that he found me...and wanted me, at least for now. "Yes, sir. I'd like that, Daddy."

Harris growled and then kissed me again, wrapping his strong hand around my cock and holding it against his. He was so much thicker than me, pressing over my entire length as I immediately began to harden. "Good boy."

A shiver ran down my spine as he thrust harder and faster, bringing us both closer to a climax. A third for me, which I didn't even know was possible. "Does that mean that if I'm a bad boy, I'll be punished?"

Harris sucked in a breath and pressed against me as a warmth spread over my hips from his seed pouring out onto me.

Digging my fingertips into his strong arms, I let go of my insecurities and came again, spewing my come with his over his strong fist.

We both held still, trying to catch our breath before he stepped back so the water could clean us up again.

"I'll never hurt you, but I do expect my boy to behave and follow the rules we put in place."

I stepped out of the spray and reached for a towel. "Rules?"

13

HARRIS

I grabbed the towel before he could get it and held it up for him to step into. I wrapped it completely around him, locking his arms around his sides like a burrito and gave him a quick kiss. "Yes, rules. But only those we agree to... and only if you want them. You don't owe me anything, and you never have to do anything you're not comfortable with." I lowered the towel so he could slip his arms out and then tied it in place under his armpits. "Let's get dressed and we can talk about it...or we can talk about it in the morning. There's no rush."

The change in Jesse was instant. He went from lazily sated to anxious and afraid. "Okay." He started walking out of the bathroom, slowly shuffling away from me.

"Jesse, sweetheart." I picked up the boxer briefs he'd brought in earlier and held them from my finger. "Would you like to put these on?"

His eyes narrowed like it was a trick question. "Do you want me to?"

Goddammit. I was already fucking this up. I blew out a deep breath and nodded. "I think you'll be more comfortable in these for right now. May I help you?"

He nodded and took a step toward me as I kneeled down and held open the waistband in front of him. Jesse slowly raised one foot up and slipped it through the leg hole, then did the same for the other. Without completely exposing him, I shimmied the boxers up his thighs and gently over his cock so he was fully covered. "Better?"

He shrugged, still unsure about the change in our status. "Yes, thank you."

This wasn't at all how I wanted the rest of the night to play out. "Okay, are you ready to go back to sleep?"

"I don't think I'll be able to sleep until I understand what you want."

I pulled him against my chest and held him. He was beginning to shiver from the chill in the air. "Okay, in your room or on the sofa?"

He bit his lip, thinking about it for a moment. "In my bed should be okay."

"Why don't you go get settled while I run upstairs and get dressed."

Jesse opened his mouth like he was going to object, but seemed to think better of it and just scurried off to his room.

I didn't like the sudden change in his demeanor.

He was obviously afraid of me now that I had mentioned rules, and fear was the last thing I ever wanted to invoke in him. I hoped to stir up a lot of emotions in Jesse over time, but never fear. I took the stairs two at a time and quickly slipped on a pair of sweats and a T-shirt.

Jesse and I both needed to have a level head for this conversation, not be distracted by whatever lust or attraction he might be feeling.

I had to remind myself of that too.

When I walked into Jesse's room, he was sitting up in bed with Luna over his thighs in her usual protective position. Well, I tried to convince myself that she was being protective of him, but I thought she was just needy and liked to keep her litter mates close to her...and Jesse was her litter mate.

"I brought you water, but I can make you some tea or cocoa if you'd like." I held out a bottle of water to Jesse.

"Water's fine." He took it and smiled bashfully, less afraid of me now. "Thank you."

"Is it okay if I sit here?" I smoothed down a corner of the comforter at the edge of the bed.

His eyes locked with mine. "Yeah. I'd invite you to sit up here, but Luna didn't leave much space."

"She never does." I sat down and rested my hand on his crossed ankles. "So, are you ready to tell me what you were so upset about earlier?"

He furrowed a brow in confusion. "My dream? I told you."

"Not your dream. After the shower. You went from what seemed to be happy to upset and...maybe even scared of me." I gave his leg a gentle shake to let him know I wasn't mad. "Can you tell me why?"

"I wasn't scared." He was looking down at his laced fingers but then met my gaze. "I guess I was a little... worried, I don't know why."

"Fair enough." I thought about how to push him for answers without breaking our fragile bond. "Was it because I mentioned rules? That word seemed to trigger you."

He was quiet for a while but then agreed with me. "Yeah, I think it was. I was just surprised, I guess. You're always so good to me, taking care of me and everything. But when there are rules, that means there's punishment and disappointment. And then you said…"

He looked away, focusing on the closet door and avoiding eye contact with me. "What did I say?"

He closed his eyes tight for a moment then sighed. "Well, you said I didn't owe you anything and I didn't have to do anything…" His eyes were glassy when he glanced at me. "Like you didn't want me anymore."

What? I couldn't follow his logic, but that didn't matter. Whether I understood what he was feeling or thinking wasn't the issue. All that mattered was making it better. "I'm so sorry you thought that." I scooted higher on the mattress, nudging Luna's big head out of the way so I was thigh to thigh with him. "I haven't done a good job of communicating with you, and that ends now."

The hope in him was apparent, despite the tear that escaped from his left eye. "What's ending?"

Apparently, I was exceptionally bad at words. "Okay, I'm just gonna lay it all out there." I had never been particularly wordy, but this was too important to fuck up by being self-conscious or subtle. Jesse needed clarification before he made any decisions. He deserved to fully understand what I was offering, even though I wasn't entirely sure myself until the words started flowing. "I am very attracted to you. Not just physically, but you're kind and sweet and respectful. All the things I look for in a boy." I paused there to give him a moment for that to sink in.

"So, you are a Daddy? Like, a real one. Not just in name during sex?"

I grinned at his adorable way of describing what had always felt like an extremely complicated lifestyle. "I am a Daddy by nature, looking for a boy...both in and out of the bedroom. Do you understand what that means?"

He nodded tentatively and then cocked an eyebrow. "Do you want me to wear diapers and sleep in a crib?"

"Not at all." Age play was part of the kink for many Daddies and boys, but that wasn't my thing. "I want you to be exactly as you are. I can't think of a single thing I'd ask you to change."

"Really?" He lowered one hand so it was in the space between our thighs. "But what did you mean by rules?"

I took his hint and reached for his hand, interlacing our fingers and holding it on my lap. "Well, right now, as my house guest, you have some rules, right? I asked you to always be honest with me and to lock the house up when you leave."

"Yeah, but those are just regular house rules. Are there any...bedroom rules?" He was tentative, but I could see the genuine interest in his eyes. "Other than calling you Daddy?"

I loved seeing his neck turn red and blossom all the way up to his ears whenever he was embarrassed. He was so beautiful. With my free hand, I traced the edge of his ear and down his jawline. I held his chin between my thumb and pointer finger as I leaned forward and gave him a kiss. "Every time I hear you say that, my dick gets hard and my heart beats faster."

He followed my retreating lips, trying to kiss me longer. We'd get there soon enough, but we needed to focus. "I like getting your dick hard...Daddy."

"Fuck, boy." I pressed my chest against his, pinning his upper body in place against the headboard until we were both gasping for breath. "We need to get through this conversation before anything else happens. Can you be a good boy?"

His Adam's apple bobbed as he swallowed back his desire. "Yes, Daddy. I can be good."

"I know you can." I had to shake my head to remember what we were just talking about. "So, that turns me the fuck on, and I'd love for you to call me Daddy in bed, but you can do it any time, if you're comfortable with that. If not, only during sex is okay."

Jesse pulled our connected hands to his chest and nodded. "Okay, I'm fine with that. Are there other rules?"

"Not really." My thumb drew circles on the back of his hand. "More than anything, I want to take care of you, and I want you to let me. It's not a rule, and you never have to do anything you don't want to do. I'll always respect your wishes and stop immediately if you ask me to. But I'll do everything I can to keep your trust and respect and would love to be the man you rely on for things. Not just for now..."

Forever was on the tip of my tongue, but I kept that to myself. It was too soon to make such a promise or declaration. Besides, I wanted Jesse to be fully comfortable with submitting to me before he was committing to me.

14

JESSE

Yes, a thousand times yes. At least, that was what my brain was screaming. But I somehow found the wherewithal to keep my mouth shut until I could get a better handle on what my brain was so enthusiastic about.

Harris was everything I'd ever wanted in a partner, and he wanted me to be his. How could that even be possible?

I'd been in submissive relationships my whole life, but submitting to Harris wasn't like what I was used to. With Harris, it was easy and natural and...safe. Safer than anything I'd ever agreed to before. Not that I'd ever really been given the option to agree or not agree. I was always just told that I would submit.

This was different.

"Yes, Harris. I want you to be my Daddy, and I want to be your boy. At least, I want to try. I'll probably screw up a lot, but if you tell me what you want, I promise to try to be good for you."

Harris's eyes fluttered closed as he inhaled, and then he looked right at me. "I promise to take care of you and meet your needs as often as I can. But if I miss something or am doing something wrong, especially if it scares you, please promise to tell me. I want this to work, Jesse. I really do."

Only a few inches separated us as I leaned forward, claiming his lips in a soft kiss. Our shower had emboldened me, and I felt empowered to not only ask for what I wanted but to take it.

Unfortunately, the adrenaline from my nightmare and the endorphins from my multiple orgasms were taking their toll, and I had to pull away from his mouth to yawn.

"Am I boring you already?" Harris kissed my earlobe then gave it a nip. "Or is it finally bedtime for my tired boy?"

I didn't ever want this moment to end, but I was crashing fast. "I think it's bedtime."

"I think that's a good decision." Harris stood up and lifted the covers so I could scoot down, redistributing Luna's weight as I went. As soon as my head was on the pillow, he kissed my temple, letting his lips linger on my skin. "Good night, my sweet boy. I'll see you in the morning."

I was so tired that my eyes closed, and I could barely say good night to Harris as he was leaving the room. But the moment he was gone, I was wide awake again.

I didn't want to sleep alone. Not after the nightmare I'd experienced earlier. And definitely not after the night we shared.

But he didn't even hint that he was willing to sleep in my bed. And he certainly didn't invite me to join him in his.

Resigned to sleep in fits and starts, I flipped over to my other side and squeezed my eyes shut. It felt like hours had passed, but when I checked the clock, Harris had only been gone for four minutes.

It was going to be a long night.

But maybe it didn't have to be. Maybe I needed to use my words and test just how good of a Daddy he was by telling him what I wanted.

After a few more minutes of internal debate, I slipped out from under the comforter wearing just my boxers and T-shirt and headed to the stairs. I'd never actually ventured upstairs before, but I'd seen Harris come out of the room directly above mine, so I was pretty sure that was his room.

The stairs were smooth and silent as I ascended, carefully centering my weight so they didn't squeak and announce my arrival. But by the time I hit the fifth riser, Luna had figured out my plan and went barreling past me and straight into Harris's room.

I knew she'd found him when I heard the telltale "*oof*" that always followed one of her body flops.

"Dammit, dog. You need to learn about personal space."

No longer bothering to be sneaky, I rushed up the rest of the stairs and peeked into the bedroom.

Harris was staring right at me with a grin. "Would you like to sleep with us, Jesse?"

I nodded and took a few steps toward him, not sure where to go.

He snapped his fingers and pointed to the foot of the bed. "Luna, move."

The dog groaned as she army crawled to the foot of the bed, obviously annoyed by the request.

Harris grabbed the top edge of his covers and lifted them, making space for me to hop in.

I didn't waste any time as I leapt right into the warm space beside him, instantly wrapping myself over his heated skin.

His bare, heated skin.

When his cock started to swell under my knee cap, I knew I was probably being bad.

"Sorry." I straightened out in the space beside Harris with only my head on his folded arm. "You're just so warm."

His big arm closed around me, repositioning me so I was fully lying on his torso. "Never apologize for touching me or arousing me. I can't help the way I respond to you any more than you can help being so damn sweet and sexy."

The flush of blood I always felt when he complimented me didn't stay in my neck long because it was needed in other regions.

He rubbed a circle over my back and then placed his hand in the center, holding me firmly in place. "But tonight, we sleep. We both need it."

I wasn't sure I'd ever sleep again.

15

HARRIS

Once Jesse settled on my chest, all the worry and tension from the night just washed away. He wanted to at least try to be my boy, and that gave me something I hadn't had for a very long time.

Hope for a future.

I had been existing on autopilot for so long, resigned to the fact that maybe there wasn't someone out there just for me.

But he was fragile, and I needed to take things slowly.

We couldn't really know how compatible we were until we actually tried to live our lives together. But I also wanted him to fully process and deal with the feelings from his past relationships. He'd been through a lot in a short period of time and one week of safety didn't seem like enough time for him to be ready to really consider something serious.

And I wanted something serious. And permanent.

So, for the next several days, our routine didn't change much. I still fussed over him in every way he'd let me, but nothing else was different. Except for the fact that he didn't go back to the guest room.

My room was now his room too.

Even Luna loved the new arrangement. She seemed relieved to have her body on both of ours at night, so neither of us could move once she landed on us. The only reason I allowed her to continue the ridiculous habit was because it kept Jesse and me from getting carried away at night. As much as I wanted to try everything with him, we both needed some boundaries for the short term.

Almost a week later, on Thursday evening, I got home from work and noticed Jesse seemed restless. Antsy.

"Is everything okay?" I patted the cushion next to me on the couch, and he reluctantly sat down.

"I guess. I just feel..." He looked around anxiously, like he wasn't sure what to do or say next. "Well, like I should be doing something. I've always had stuff to do whether I wanted to or not, and it's weird to just do nothing all day."

I mentally kicked myself for not anticipating that this would be a problem. Not that I could read minds or that I proclaimed to know what he was thinking at every moment, but he'd mentioned a few times that he wanted to help and keep busy.

And I ignored him. Not intentionally ignored him, but didn't hear his offer as the request it actually was. Fuck, I needed to do better.

"Well, that's easy to remedy. Maybe if you have some chores around the house, that'll help keep you busy."

He nodded quickly. "Yeah, I think that would be good. Also...maybe I can get a job."

"Of course. Whenever you're ready, I know several people who own companies that would be happy to hire you. Even Tony mentioned needing some help over at the clinic."

Jesse's eyes perked up, and his shoulders dropped with relief. "I'm so glad you're okay with this. I was afraid you wouldn't let me."

"Let you?" I pulled him onto my lap and wrapped my arms around his waist. "First of all, I don't control you. I will never *not* let you do something. All I want is for you to be happy, and if working and being productive makes you happy, then I will encourage you and support you in any way I can. Do you understand?"

He had a bashful grin on his face as he peeked at me from under long lashes. "Yes, Daddy." He didn't use the term outside the bedroom very often, and when he did, a soft flush always crept up his neck.

And I never got tired of hearing it.

"Good boy." I nestled my face into the crook of his neck and gave him a kiss by his ear. "You make me very happy."

He turned and threw his arms around my neck, embracing me tightly as the tension in his body released.

I just held him for a few long moments, enjoying the quiet happiness we both radiated. But when his stomach rumbled, I knew it was time to get moving. "I didn't pick up dinner tonight because I was thinking maybe we could go out."

Jesse pulled away, and his eyes got big. "Like on a date? In a restaurant?"

I poked his side and gave him a tickle. "Yes, in a restaurant. I'll even put on a nice sweater since you pretty much only see me in work clothes and sweats."

He pulled back and tugged the hemline of my T-shirt. "I like you in your work clothes. You're all sexy and manly and...stinky."

I laughed and lifted him off my lap and dropped him onto the couch beside me. "Fine, fine. I can take a hint. I'll go shower and change. I'll be ready in...twenty minutes?"

Jesse stood up and then cocked his head, looking back at me. "I'm not sure I have anything to wear that's... nice. How fancy are we talking?"

"Not fancy. I'm thinking pizza or burgers. Something casual, so a T-shirt will be fine." I gave him a kiss on his nose before turning toward the stairs. "We'll go shopping this weekend. Make sure you have a full wardrobe for job-hunting and date nights."

"Date nights?" He tested the words with a big grin. "I like the sound of that."

———

My boy looked good in everything and nothing, but when he was excited, he absolutely glowed.

It was a clear night, so we decided to bundle up and walk the four blocks to one of my favorite burger joints instead of driving downtown. It was a cool night, but Jesse wrapped his arms around my bicep for warmth, hanging off me as we walked.

I loved every second of it.

"Is that a dog park?" He looked out in the distance, pointing to an open field.

"Not officially. The city owns it and lots of neighbors do use it as a dog park, but I've also seen kids playing baseball and soccer out there when the weather's nice."

Jesse looked at me with his big eyes. "Can I bring Luna there tomorrow?"

"Of course." There was a twinge in my belly, that I didn't like the idea of him being out in the world by himself, but I didn't dare verbalize that fear. He was a grown-ass man who had taken care of himself long before I came along. He could handle himself at a dog park. "She would love that."

I could tell by the way he hopped beside me, giddy in delight, that he would love that too.

16

JESSE

Harris made a list of basic chores for me to complete and stuck it to the fridge with a magnet. They weren't hard things to accomplish, but knowing he wanted me to get them done, and then actually doing them, filled me with a sense of pride I'd never felt before.

No one had ever really trusted me to be responsible.

Bruce told me to clean the trailer and cook him meals, but he was a disgusting slob, so the second he walked in the door, our cluttered space was a mess again. He never acknowledged my efforts or appreciated the results. He just liked exerting power over me. Making me do stuff he thought I wouldn't enjoy was merely an extension of his abuse.

Harris wasn't like that.

The first day I had my list, I spent the entire day meticulously dry-mopping the floor of all the dog hair, making our bed with the tightest corners I could muster, and cooking a three-course meal that was palatable but not particularly good.

And he gushed over every inch of the house, telling me how proud he was and what a good job I did. Truthfully, he went a little overboard, but I knew it was coming from a good place. He wanted me to feel appreciated. And I did.

I also felt loved.

Neither of us had said the word, and I wasn't sure he ever would. But that was the warm feeling that radiated from me every time he was around. The safety and care I received from Harris couldn't be described in any other way.

After Harris and I had lunch on Friday, I did a final sweep of the house to make sure it was nice and tidy before I put Luna on the leash, and we headed out.

Her butt didn't stop wiggling as we walked down the street. She was so excited that she wanted to pull forward and run, but I used the commands Harris taught me to make her heel and not pull on her lead.

Once we got inside the gate at the field, I saw a few other dogs running around. She couldn't contain her excitement, so I let her off the leash.

Like a bat out of hell, Luna took off at full speed. For the first few minutes, she just ran around aimlessly, sniffing the ground and exploring every blade of grass and pile of poop.

At least until she found an old tennis ball. Once she had that, she picked it up and brought it to me to throw for her. It didn't take long for me to regret not bringing gloves with me. By the second time she brought me her ball, it was a slimy, muddy mess. But she was so happy to play that I couldn't deny her. "I'm gonna need two showers after this, girl. I hope you appreciate it."

"She does." A guy my age had walked up beside me, holding a long piece of plastic with a cup at the end. "But you might want to look into one of these chucking sticks. It'll save your hand."

"Oh, hi." I took a look at his stick. "What is that?"

Just then, an older golden retriever trotted over with a ball in his mouth. When the guy lowered the stick, the dog dropped the ball right into the cup at the end and watched attentively as the man flicked the stick and sent the ball flying across the park. "A chucking stick. So you can throw farther without having to actually touch the ball."

"I definitely need one of those." Luna was back with her slime ball, so I picked it up between two fingers and lobbed it as far as I could get it. "Can I take a picture of that to show my..." I hesitated, not exactly sure how to describe Harris. Boyfriend was on the tip of my tongue, but then Daddy also came to mind. "Um, Luna's owner."

"Yeah, sure." He held out the stick while I pulled the phone Harris gave me out and snapped a picture. "My name is Jason. Are you a dog-walker too?"

Dog-walker? That was when I realized there were two other dogs circling nearby that seemed to be with Jason. "Oh, no. I'm just helping out a...friend." I didn't like the way that word tasted, but I didn't think too much about it. "I'm Jesse."

"Good to meet you, Jesse. I haven't seen you out here before. Are you new to the area?"

"Yeah, I just moved here a couple weeks ago. We're a few blocks over."

"Oh, cool. Well, welcome." Since my hand was gross, he held up his fist for me to bump with my clean hand. "If you're interested in a dog-walking gig, I can probably hook you up. My uncle has a company that matches owners and walkers, and he's always looking for more walkers."

"Really? Actually, I am looking for a job, but I've never considered walking dogs. Does it require any experience?"

"Nah. Nothing more than what you already have." He slipped his hand into his pocket and pulled out a business card. "Here's my card. You can go to the website and sign up as a walker. Make sure you list me as your referral. I'll let my uncle know to look for your application."

The idea of making some money while playing with Luna and other dogs sounded pretty good. "What does it pay?"

"The hourly rate is about ten bucks per dog, but if you have a few dogs at a time, that adds up. Also, if the dogs are happy and well-exercised, most of the owners will give nice tips." He waggled his eyebrows at me almost suggestively, but I thought he just had a playful personality. "At least that's been my experience."

I'd only ever worked in minimum-wage jobs, so $20 or $30 an hour sounded pretty good. And if I could handle more dogs, that would be amazing. "So, you're getting paid $30 right now to be here?"

He smiled and shook his head. "I've got five dogs here." Those two over there, these two lingering behind me, and Trooper."

Trooper deposited his ball into the chucking stick again and waited for Jason to throw.

"Last time. We've got to get the girls home, old man." He threw the ball, and Trooper went flying after it with Luna hot on his heels. Unfortunately for the old dog, Luna got to the ball first and headed back before poor Trooper even realized the ball wasn't out there any more.

"Sorry about that. I definitely need to get her out here more often."

"No worries. She can keep the ball. We've got to run anyway, but call me if you have any questions. And even if you decide not to apply for a job, I'm out here a few times a day, so if you ever wanna meet up, just let me know."

"Thanks, Jason." I waved as he ran to the end of the fence to round up his canine crew. "I will."

My smile was ridiculously wide as I continued playing with Luna. Not only had I possibly lined up a job that paid well, but I might've made a new friend. I'd never been good at making friends, and Jason seemed like a pretty normal guy.

When Luna finally got tired of fetching the ball and decided to investigate a set of beagles that had arrived, I fired off a text to Harris with a photo of the chucking stick. ***I think I need one of these.***

I watched the response bubbles pop up immediately and then disappear, and I wondered if maybe he was mad that I was asking for something. I quickly typed out a follow-up text. ***You don't have to buy it. I just mean, when I make some money, I'm getting one of these. Luna found a ball and it's very slimy.*** I added a laughing emoji to make sure he knew I was joking around.

Oh, the plastic ball thrower?

Yeah. A dog-walker at the park had one, and he didn't have to touch anything gross to play with his dogs. I snapped a picture of my muddy hand and sent it to Harris. ***Unlike myself.***

Harris immediately responded back with a laughing emoji of his own. **I'll pick one up on the way home, unless you want to go with me to the pet store.**

I wouldn't mind going to the store. That could be fun.

17

HARRIS

"A chucking stick." I shook my head and laughed at myself. "I'm an idiot."

Cort flipped up his welding helmet and looked at me. "What are you laughing at? Am I on fire again?"

I glanced down at his pant legs to make sure then shook my head.

"Then what's so funny?"

I flipped up my helmet too. I didn't really want to get into this with Cort, but he knew about Jesse and was one of the few people I could be open with. "Jesse sent me a picture of some guy holding one of those ball launcher toys for dogs. He said he wanted one of those, and I thought he was talking about the guy holding the stick."

Cort threw back his head and howled. "Damn, that must've freaked you out."

"Kinda. I mean, he's much closer to Jesse's age, so I wouldn't be surprised if he was interested in a cute little twink, but..."

Cort cocked his head and smiled. "But you love him, right? No-plans-to-let-him-go kind of deal."

Was I that transparent? "Would it be weird if I said yes?"

"No, of course not. I've never seen you this happy before. I could've told you from day one that this kid was it for you."

"I certainly hope he agrees."

"So, he's not into the guy from the dog park?"

"No, he was talking about the dog toy. Apparently Luna's ball was really slimy. Anyway, Jesse is just... He's just so...perfect. I can't help but wonder if he'll get bored with me."

Cort took a deep breath and turned off the welder so he could focus his attention on me. "Look, I haven't met the guy, so I can't say for sure. But, if he's making you this happy, I'm sure you do the same for him. Not everybody is comfortable with the Daddy/boy dynamic. So if you guys are compatible in that way, I think you should just focus on continuing to build from there."

I gripped the back of my neck and stretched out my muscles. "Yeah, I know you're right. I'm not gonna screw it up this time."

Cort reached over and patted my knee. "I know you won't, big guy. You got this. And even if he does dump you for some twink from the dog park, at least you'll have these memories."

My jaw clenched, and I was ready to punch Cort in the face when he started to laugh. He held up his hands in surrender. "Joking, I'm joking. Sheesh, you need to get laid or something."

Yeah, I do. We'd been taking things slow, but that might've been creating a different kind of tension in me. At least that was something I knew how to rectify.

When I got home, the house was spotless, and Jesse had just hopped in the shower. Through the curtain, he explained that he decided to take Luna for a run after the dog park and wanted to wash off the sweat.

His clothes were in a heap next to the shower, so I picked them up and carried them to the hamper. As usual, I slipped my hand into each pocket to make sure he hadn't left anything in them that didn't need to get washed. I'd lost more than a few key fobs and important notes before I got into this routine. What I didn't expect to find was a business card in his back pocket.

As soon as I saw it, that weird knot in my gut was back. Jason Millionia. Million-Hair Dog Walking Service. He had to be the guy from the park.

I didn't want to draw any conclusions, but my mood suddenly took a downward turn.

Of course, I'd meant what I said about not forcing Jesse into anything. He was free to be friends with anyone he wanted. And if he wanted to be more than friends with anyone, that was his choice too. I just hoped that wasn't the case. But, since we'd never specifically talked about it, that was a conversation we'd have to have sooner rather than later.

―――――

"Is this enough?" I gestured to the assortment of fetch toys and bones for Luna overflowing from a basket. "Considering we came here for one toy."

Jesse tried to look innocent as he held up a stuffed zebra. "Just one more and we're good. I promise."

I sighed. "Put it in the basket."

"I promise I'll pay you back as soon as I get my first paycheck." He grabbed the basket from my arm and headed to the cashier. "And business supplies might be a write-off, right? Also...what's a write-off?"

I chuckled and pulled out my card so he could use the self-checkout aisle. "I don't know for sure, but don't worry about it. Consider these a congratulations-on-your-new-job gift."

"I like how that sounds." He leaned up on his tiptoes to give me a chaste kiss. Our first real PDA. Then he whispered in my ear, "Thank you, Daddy."

I swatted his bottom and waggled my eyebrows. "You're gonna get me in trouble for indecent exposure in here if you keep that up."

He giggled and started swiping the items across the scanner. "But I don't actually have a new job yet. They might not hire me. If they don't, Luna will get these all to herself."

I stood right beside him, pressing my hip against his as I took the items he'd just scanned and loaded them into a bag like it was a Jenga game. "They would be stupid not to hire you. You're perfect."

Jesse sucked in a stuttering breath and bit his lip as he turned to me. "I am?"

I nodded and brushed a soft kiss over his lips. "You definitely are."

18

JESSE

Dog-walking was the best job in the world. I wondered why everyone wasn't doing it. Even after just a few days, I knew I'd want to do it forever. I could make a hundred bucks a day in a couple hours and with only two or three dogs at a time, so I still had plenty of time to do my chores and make dinner for Harris before he got home.

Harris didn't add dinner as a requirement on my chore list, but he seemed to appreciate being able to come straight home after a long day without having to stop and pick up takeout. Also, it was cheaper and healthier to cook at home, so I was happy to do it.

I still wasn't a great cook, but I found a few websites for beginners in the kitchen and was learning how to put together one-pot meals that were quite tasty. Harris said everything was good, but I could tell he really meant it for some of the dishes. Those were worked into the weekly meal plan, and a few nights were left open for takeout or restaurants.

Harris insisted on going on a proper date at least once a week. We'd both get dressed in nicer clothes than we wore during the day and either walked to a local place or drove downtown. It was always a fun way to catch up on how things were going and just enjoy being together.

My job paid me daily, including bonuses for picking up "drop-in" walks and accepting special requests, so I actually had a somewhat steady income coming in. For the first time in my life, I could buy stuff.

And other than Luna, I had no one to shop for but Harris.

"It's just something little." He didn't seem like the senti-mental type, but as soon as we sat down in the restaurant, I pulled out a small box and handed it to him. "It's silly."

He accepted the box and raised an eyebrow at me. "It's not my birthday."

"I know." I wasn't planning to remind him that it had been exactly one month since he saved me. It felt like a

lifetime had passed since that fateful night. But everything changed for me once Bruce was permanently out
of my life, and I wanted Harris to know how much I
appreciated him and what he'd done for me. "But I saw
it and immediately thought of you."

His face was stoic as he carefully slipped the ribbon off
the box and lifted the top. His breath hitched when he
looked inside. "Jesse..."

I could feel the emotion radiating off him from across the
table. There wasn't an easy way to reach for his hand
while he held the box, so I wrapped my ankles around
his, locking him in place.

He looked up at me with a smile then lifted the silver
keychain from the box. "'World's Best Daddy,' huh?"

I nodded. "Yep. And look at the back."

He turned it over and saw the photo of me and Luna
etched into metal. "It's amazing. I love it."

Just holding him by the ankles wasn't enough, so I
scooted my chair around the table until I was right
beside him, close enough for him to pull me against his
chest in a tight squeeze.

"You're amazing, Jesse. In every way." He pressed his lips to my temple and held them for a moment before dropping his forehead there. "I love you."

Now it was my turn to get emotional. My eyes immediately met his, and I could feel the sincerity in his stare. "I love you too."

Harris leaned down and kissed me hard, crashing into me with so much heat that I was starting to sweat despite the cool restaurant air. "Do you want to get out of here?"

"Yes, please." I vaguely heard him saying something to the waiter as he pulled out some cash and dropped it onto the table, but I didn't pay attention.

Harris loved me. And I loved him.

We were in love.

Everything I'd been worried about seemed so insignificant now that we'd said the words out loud. Deep down, I felt his love every day. Everything he did for me screamed of it, but I was still waiting to hear the words. And now that I had, I wanted to give myself to him fully.

For weeks, I'd been trying to get more than the occasional handjob out of him, but he wanted to wait. Wanted to make sure I was ready to make a long-term decision. I'd been ready, but now he finally seemed to believe me.

Without saying it, we were rushing out of that restaurant to get home so we could fuck. I almost couldn't walk because I was so hard, even though a tiny bit of me was scared because he was so thick. I'd only had sex with a handful of guys and none of them were particularly big. Not even close to what Harris was packing.

But I wanted to feel him tear me open and claim me as his. I wasn't at all afraid that he wouldn't be gentle or patient with me as I got used to him.

My Daddy always knew what I needed.

As soon as we were in the car, I reached for his hand and looked at his profile while he was driving. "We're finally doing it, right? Tonight?"

Harris chuckled and pulled my hand to his lips to drop a kiss there. "Fuck, I hope so. My balls are so blue, I feel like that bubble gum girl from Willy Wonka."

"Violet Beauregarde?" I busted up in laughter. "Did you actually equate your balls to giant blueberries?"

He just shrugged with a completely straight face. "I'm just warning you. I might need to triple bag it just to catch it all."

"I'm not sure it works that way." I rested my head on his shoulder. "We should have gotten tested, huh?"

Harris tensed and then shook his head. "Dammit, you're right. I should have thought of that sooner. I'm sorry, baby. That's my fault."

I loved when he called me that. It was rare because he usually reserved that particular endearment for when I was upset about something, which wasn't very often anymore. Other than the occasional nightmare or when I accidentally broke something, I was almost always happy. "I can make an appointment to see Tony, if you'd like."

He turned and gave me a quick kiss on my nose without taking his eyes off the road. "Yes, please. Make one for me too. I'll go after work on any day he's available. The sooner the better."

I giggled. "We'll survive with condoms for a few times."

He sighed as if that was such a hardship. "I guess you're right." He squeezed my hand again then placed mine over his cock. "You're worth it."

19

HARRIS

The entire drive was less than eight minutes, but it felt like an eternity as red light after red light kept us away from our bed. After hearing him say that he loved me, my cock was painfully hard and getting naked with him was my singular focus.

Yes, I wanted to be inside him, and I definitely wanted to climax while I was there, but just being with him, my entire body touching his entire body, was truly what motivated me every day. It was the only reason I was able to wait an entire month before even considering penetration.

Because he was enough for me, even without the sex.

But fuck, I really wanted the sex too.

When we pulled up to the house, Jesse jumped out of the truck and practically ran up the porch to the door. "Are you coming or what?" He looked back at me, impatiently holding open the front door while Luna jumped all over him.

"I just need to grab something. I'll be right in." I waited for Jesse to walk away from the entryway to put Luna out back, then I grabbed the pink box from the back of my truck. I had picked it up on my way home from work and hid it under my gym bag.

He wasn't the only one who remembered our one-month anniversary.

I locked the front door and headed straight upstairs with my surprise while Jesse waited for Luna to come back in. Once the box was tucked under a flannel shirt, I took off my socks and shoes then got completely undressed before slipping into bed. I barely had the sheet over my waist when Jesse ran into the room, breathless.

"Don't start without me." He ripped his shirt over his head and almost fell on his face trying to hop out of his jeans.

I smiled at his eagerness because I was just as eager. "Slow down there, boy. I don't want to end up in the ER tonight because you couldn't get naked fast enough."

He didn't slow down as he continued to fumble out of his clothing. "Fast enough? I waited an entire month for this moment. I'm allowed to be excited."

"Just don't hurt yourself."

Instead of hopping into bed on his side, he sprang forward and landed on my lap, straddling my thighs as he wrapped his arms around my neck and claimed my mouth in a sloppy kiss.

His aggressive kissing was playful at first, but it quickly turned heated, and it was time I took control of the situation.

With a few quick moves, I flipped us both over and placed him on the sheet so he was beneath me, his thighs still spread on either side of my folded legs.

I had imagined a very slow and romantic first time between us, but neither of us had the patience for that. We just needed to be connected as fully and as quickly as possible.

I yanked open my nightstand drawer and grabbed a few condoms and the lube as I looked at his beautiful body beneath me. "You're so fucking sexy. Thank you for trusting me."

He reached for my cock and began to quickly stroke me. "Please, Daddy. I need you inside me."

I kissed his neck, trying to slow things down as my hands trailed from his chest, down his hips, and eventually around to his pert ass.

When I squeezed his soft skin, we both moaned in anticipation.

"Tell me this is mine, boy."

"Yes." He rolled his pelvis up, trying to get friction on his cock against my belly.

I licked the rim of his ear. "Yes, what?"

"Yes, Daddy. My ass is yours. All yours." He wiggled in my hands. "Now take it already."

I gently nipped at his chin before sliding down his body, dropping kisses over his sternum and around his nipples, trailing all the way down to the head of his wet dick. "Looks like you're the one starting without me."

"I can't help it." He rolled his hips again. "I feel like I might come just from looking at you."

Good answer. I flicked the head of his cock with my tongue, lapping up the bead of moisture forming there. "You taste so good for Daddy."

His back arched, and he tried to push farther into my mouth, but it wasn't time for that. Yet.

I lightly smacked one ass cheek and then flattened my tongue around the head of his dick before dragging down to his balls. I wanted to spend hours with him in my mouth like that, but neither of us could hold out much longer.

Instead, I lifted his lower back with my fingertips, angling him so his pink hole was staring right at me. My eyes met his as the realization of what I was about to do dawned on him.

His lips slowly parted like he was about to speak, but no words came out. He just lay there, staring at me with a slack jaw as I lowered my face against his warm center and poked my tongue into his opening.

"Oh, shit." He sucked in a deep breath, and his whole body tightened for a moment before he pressed against me, urging me deeper.

Everything about him was perfect. The way he felt. The way he smelled. And definitely the way he tasted.

I fucked into his ass with my mouth, loosening him up before slipping my middle finger inside beneath my tongue.

Jesse's breathing was uneven, but I could tell he liked what I was doing because every time I backed away, he followed my movements, trying to keep the connection between us.

I kissed his taint and slowly moved back up his body as I reached for the lube.

Once my mouth was back on his, I kept it there as I lubed up my fingers and continued to work him open.

He squirmed below me, whimpering with need. "I think I'm close, Daddy. It feels so good."

He seemed worried about what might happen, so I removed my fingers and focused on bringing him back down for the next few minutes. "You're okay, baby. I won't be disappointed by anything that happens. It's all perfect."

He took in a stuttering breath and glanced down at my hand. "You're not done, right?"

I chuckled as I handed him a condom. "I've barely gotten started, boy. Can you help me with this?"

The way he fumbled with the condom was reminiscent of a virgin on prom night. But I knew this wasn't his first time. Maybe he just wasn't used to the kind of attention

I was giving him, but he managed to get it tightly fitted over my length while still leaving plenty of room at the front for the huge load I promised him.

Once I was safely bagged, I put some more lube on my hand and worked it over myself and his opening before getting positioned over him and kissing him again. "I love you. You're being a very good boy for Daddy."

His breath hitched, and his cock bounced against my belly. "I love you too, Daddy. Will you finally make me yours?"

Hovering just inches above his face so I could watch every expression, I pushed against his opening until he relaxed enough to take my full length in.

His breaths were ragged, and he had to take a moment to get acclimated to the intrusion. I'd heard complaints from prior lovers that I was too wide for comfort, and I didn't want this to hurt Jesse in any way. After a minute or two, he slowly exhaled and opened his eyes. "I'm good now." He tapped my hip. "You can move."

I grinned but didn't say anything else as I slowly pulled out and then pushed back into him. He was so tight. It had been a while for me, but I couldn't remember ever feeling that kind of iron grip around my cock.

"Are you sure you're okay?"

He nodded and reached for his dick. "Oh, yeah. I'm almost there again."

Well, shit. I started to move faster, sliding in and out of him with shallow strokes.

It didn't take long for both of us to be covered in sweat and breathless from holding back our releases.

I stayed strong for as long as I could before finally giving in. "Come for me, boy. I want to feel you as I give you my load."

With just a few more strokes of his hand, he sprayed against my skin, convulsing from every direction. His tight channel clasped onto my cock, bringing me over the edge and milking several strong eruptions out of me.

I held perfectly still within him, relishing the fact that he'd given himself to me so completely.

When our tremors finally subsided, I gently pulled out of him and then gave him a languid kiss before slipping out of bed to get a warm towel to clean up with.

Jesse lay sprawled across the bed with the most beautiful freshly fucked glow emitting from him like the aura of an angel.

He sometimes liked to tease that I was his angel for rescuing him, but I knew the truth. That boy was sent straight to me. To save me from my demons and bring me more joy than I knew possible.

20

JESSE

I knew sex with Harris was going to be great, but I'd had no idea what great sex even meant. I'd never been with someone who cared about how I felt, much less wanted me to consider the act pleasurable. I was always just the means to someone else's end, responsible for my own release after they were passed out or gone.

But Harris wasn't like that.

Harris carefully wiped up the lube leaking from my bottom and the come drying on my skin, then wrapped me in his arms as I fell asleep on his chest. I could have stayed there forever, but my bladder had other ideas.

We slept for about an hour before I had to get up to take a piss. When I came back, Harris was sitting up in the bed, waiting for me.

"I'm sorry, did I wake you?"

He cocked his head, clearly checking me out. "No, I think my stomach woke me up."

I put my hand on my belly and frowned. "Yeah, we skipped dinner, didn't we?"

"Yeah, but if you want a snack, I have a surprise for you."

I crawled into bed beside him and raised my eyebrow. "Is this just gonna be some kind of cream-filled eclair joke?"

He laughed and pulled me up onto his lap. "Sorta, but it's not just innuendo. I actually have something for us. Want me to grab it?"

He seemed so excited that I couldn't resist agreeing. "Yeah, I love surprises."

Harris scooted me onto the mattress then grabbed a suspiciously draped shirt off the dresser, revealing a pink bakery box.

"What is that? And when did you get it?" I would've definitely noticed if snacks had been brought in at some point.

"I have my ways." He winked at me then placed the box in front of me before he slipped into bed, waiting for me to open it.

Once we were talking about it, I really was hungry. I opened the box and couldn't believe what I was seeing. There were four cupcakes, and each one had a different word written on it. The first one said "I." The second one said "love." The third one said "my." And the fourth one said "boy."

Tears immediately began to well in my eyes as I looked at Harris in disbelief. "You remembered too?

"Of course I did." He grinned and grabbed the cupcake that said boy on it. "How could I possibly forget the day you came into my life?"

———

We ended up celebrating our anniversary for the entire weekend.

By the time Sunday evening rolled around, it hurt to walk. But every ache in my body reminded me of how much I was loved.

On Monday morning, I met up with Jason at the dog park. I tried to jog over to him, but I winced, giving away my predicament.

"Someone had a good weekend." He waggled his eyebrows suggestively.

I wanted to deny it, but the telltale blush on my neck and face ruined any chance I had at discretion. "Okay, fine." I gave him a shy smile. "Yes, it was our one-month anniversary."

Jason stopped short, making all the dogs he was leading stop with him. "One month? That's it? The way you talk about this guy, I thought you guys had been together for years."

"Sometimes it feels like it. He's exactly right for me in every way, so everything is just really easy. But yeah, technically it's only been a month." And really, only a few weeks since we'd admitted our attraction to each other and allowed things to get physical.

"I need to see this guy." Jason waved his hand toward my phone. "Whoever has you this lovestruck must be super hot."

Part of me didn't want to share Harris with anybody, even Jason, but I unlocked my phone and showed him a picture I'd snapped while Harris was watching TV with Luna on his lap.

"Damn, Jesse. How do you snag a silver fox daddy like that?"

"What?" I laughed, surprised by his reference.

"I'd be his boy any day." He shook his head and sighed. "But alas, all the good ones are taken."

"Well, I don't know about all of them." I pulled my phone away before he started drooling on the screen. "But this one certainly is."

"Ohhh, someone's the jealous type." Jason nudged my shoulder and started walking again. "I would be too. You better hold on to that one."

I plan to. As we started walking, it hit me that he was talking about Daddies and boys, even though I had never mentioned that aspect of our relationship to Jason before. "So, how do you know he's my Daddy?" I said it quietly, even though nobody was within earshot of us.

"Is he?" Jason pretended to clutch imaginary pearls at the scandalous revelation. "I was just teasing, but you seriously have all the luck."

"Have you had a Daddy before?" Again, I whispered, still self-conscious about using those terms in public.

"I keep trying, but the Daddies I've hooked up with weren't quite right for me. Either too aggressive or too... weird. What they were into just wasn't what I was looking for, but I like to keep the dream alive, ya know?"

"Yeah, it's actually kinda new for me. I guess I've always been submissive, but I've never been in a relationship quite like this before."

Jason looked at me and grinned. "Is it amazing? I bet it's amazing."

I sighed happily. "It is. It really, really is."

"Okay, okay. Enough of the bragging. Let's get inside the gate so these dogs can run wild. I'm taking on a few extra shifts today to earn some extra money, so I need to wear these ones out soon so I can grab the next bunch."

"That sounds like a lot. Is everything okay?"

"Oh yeah. I'm fine. I just have a cut on my foot that might be getting infected, so I need to go see a doctor about that. Without insurance, it's gonna cost a fortune."

I thought about Harris's friend Tony and wondered if he would help. "I might know somebody who can help. I'll talk to Harris about it and let you know."

"Thanks. With as klutzy as I am, I need a good first-aid hookup."

21

HARRIS

I was just about to leave work when I had an idea. ***How does pizza sound?***

Delish. But no onions.

I grinned. No onions was because he didn't like kissing me with onion breath. ***You know I like your onion breath.***

Daaaadddy! I could picture his fake whine. I teased him about onion breath one time, and he'd refused to eat them ever since. He was freakin adorable when he was embarrassed about silly stuff. ***Get them if YOU want them. But I'm fine without.***

Obviously, I didn't get onions. As cute as it was, I never wanted Jesse to be self-conscious or shy around me. My

143

whole focus in life had evolved into making him happy and ensuring all of his physical, mental, and emotional needs were being met.

Forcing him to eat something that stressed him out was not being a good Daddy.

And that was all I wanted to be. He was my good boy, and he deserved a good Daddy.

That was why I also ran into the electronics store near the pizza place and picked up a gift for Jesse. He's been working so hard and doing his chores so well that I wanted to show him how much I appreciated him.

When I walked through the front door, Luna barreled into me, so Jesse grabbed the pizza from my hand before I dropped it, and he took it to the table he'd set for us. We usually ate lunch in front of the TV but breakfast and dinner were always at the table.

Well, usually. Pizza was often a coffee table meal, but apparently, Jesse wanted to be a bit more formal.

"The table looks nice." He had candles and a vase with cut flowers from the garden. "Did I forget an occasion?" Was it the anniversary of our first kiss...or maybe the first time he saw me naked?

"No occasion." He pulled two slices off the pie and put them on a plate for me. Then he served himself before giving me his attention again. "I just. Well, I really love and appreciate you, and I wanted to make sure you know that. I don't want to take you for granted. I'm lucky to have you, and I plan to do everything I can to keep you."

I had no idea where this conversation stemmed from, but I reached for his hand and held it firmly in mine. "You've got me, baby. You know I'm not going anywhere. And I hope you never plan to go anywhere either."

He sucked in a deep breath and then exhaled with a relieved smile. "Good."

I watched him take a bite, but he still seemed anxious. "Is everything okay? Do you want to talk about something?"

He kept his eyes on his plate as he lowered his pizza. "It's just that, I was talking to Jason today, and he was saying how you're such a hot Daddy and he'd want you... and I needed to make sure to keep you happy." He looked up at me with big eyes. "You'll tell me if I'm not making you happy anymore, right? You'll give me a chance to do better if you ever get tired of me."

"Baby." I pushed back from the table and held out my arm for him to come to my lap. "After the weekend we just had, I thought I'd made it clear that you're every-thing I've ever wanted in a boy. You're perfect for me. And I want to be perfect for you. If anything ever changes, we'll talk about it." I gently tugged his chin until he was looking right at me. "Right? We'll talk about it like we are right now."

"Yes, Daddy." He nodded as he spoke, emphasizing his sincerity. "Thank you for not getting mad at me."

I held him tightly, rocking him slightly against my chest. "I'll never get mad at you for wanting to talk something out. Even if I don't like what we're talking about, I promise to always listen and do my best to understand."

"Thank you." He was just getting up from my lap when he got excited. "Oh, I almost forgot." Jesse dropped into his chair and picked up his pizza, holding it right in front of his face without taking a bite. "Jason needs to see a doctor, but he doesn't have insurance, so he's working extra hours so he can afford it. Do you think Tony might be willing to see him?"

My head spun at the sudden change in topic, but I caught up to his new train of thought. "Yeah, of course. He'll take anyone, whether they have insurance or not."

Jesse nodded while he chewed. "Cool. Can I get his number?"

That annoying knot in my gut fluttered, but I didn't let my jealousy show. I trusted Tony with Jesse. And more importantly, I trusted Jesse with Tony. "Of course. We need to make appointments to see him anyway."

Jesse's gaze was heated and a blush crept up his neck. "Yeah, let's try to do that this week. Sooner than later."

After we ate, Jesse took up his position on the couch, and Luna was quick to claim his body as her cushion. That dog was a cock-block like no other. But my cock was tucked away for the time being because I had other plans for the night.

"While I was out, I picked up something to show you how much I appreciate all your hard work here and with the dogs." I pulled the Nintendo console out of the box and held it out to him. "I'm so proud of you, baby."

"A Nintendo Switch?" He reached for it like it was made of gold and slowly turned it around in his hands. "For me? For real?"

"Yes, for you." I gave him a kiss on the head then mussed his hair. He needed a haircut soon, but that was a topic for a different time. "You're my good boy, and you deserve a prize."

He cradled the game console to his chest and held back tears. "This is the best thing anyone has ever given me."

That broke my heart but also made me proud to be the one to do it. "Your love is the best thing anyone has ever given me, so we're even."

He placed the box on the table and wrestled out from under Luna to stand up and kiss me hard.

Within seconds, we were a jumble of lips and teeth and tongues and moans. Apparently, my cock wasn't as tucked away as I thought because it stood at full attention, ready to be warmed up by Jesse's hot little body.

EPILOGUE
JESSE (SIX MONTHS LATER)

Once the weather was nice, Luna and I started running in the afternoons. At first, it was just a way to get out her last bit of energy before Harris got home and we were inside for the night. But after the first few blocks of pain, I realized how much I enjoyed it. And after a month of nightly runs, I could stay out for an hour at a pretty quick pace without even breaking a sweat.

Okay, there was some sweat involved. Actually, a lot of sweat.

But I was stronger and healthier than I'd ever been, and life seemed to be getting better with every passing day.

Harris insisted on teaching me how to invest my earnings, but there was one critical thing I was missing to feel like a real and functional adult. I yanked open the lid to the mailbox and stuck my hand inside, hoping it was finally there.

The missing piece.

A stack of envelopes was nestled inside a folded catalog, so I pulled them all out and carefully checked each piece. Bill. Bill. Bill. Bill. Junk mail. Bill. And then I saw it. The letter from the Department of Motor Vehicles.

I tucked everything under my armpit and ran inside the house, with Luna hot on my heels. She knew something good was happening, so she ran upstairs and then quickly returned with a towel. Apparently, she'd been paying attention during our sexy times and knew we always needed a towel afterward.

I'd need to talk to Harris about getting her a bed outside of the room to wait for us to finish. Or maybe she'd like to be in the closet for a little while every night. I took the towel from her and let her kiss my cheek. "Thank you, girl. That's very helpful."

Tossing the towel aside, I carefully opened the letter and held my breath.

My driver's license.

I'd never had one before, even though I had learned how to drive when I was ten, so Harris helped me with the paperwork needed to get my license. It was something I always equated with freedom and independence, and now I finally had it.

Thanks to Harris.

Just then, the front door opened, and Harris came inside. "Hey, baby. I'm home."

I smiled and held up the little plastic card. "I got it."

Harris was beaming with pride as he scooped me into his arms and held me. "I'm so proud of you."

The kiss he gave me was slow and soft, not meant to lead to anything else. Just a transfer of his love to me.

"Thank you for making it possible."

"Let me take a look at that." He held the card up to the light, as if he needed to take a closer inspection. "It looks good, but I think they messed up one thing."

"They did?" I yanked the card out of his hand and read every line, looking for the typo. "Where?"

"Right there." He pointed to the line with my name on it. "It says Jesse Kramer."

My name was spelled right. I took a step closer to the lamp, holding it up to the light like Harris had, as if that would make the error more apparent to me. "What's wrong with it?"

When he didn't speak, I turned back and saw Harris down on one knee with a ring in his hand. "I think it should say Jesse Martins. What do you think?"

My hands flew to my open mouth as the driver's license was long forgotten. I dropped to my knees at the same time tears dropped down my cheeks. "Yes!"

I choked back a sob as Harris pulled me against his chest. "You'll really marry me and be my boy forever?"

"Yes, Daddy!" I kissed every inch of his face, laughing and crying as I did it. "Yes, infinity."

Luna quickly appeared, licking away my tears before she grabbed the towel and tossed it at Harris's face. "Geez, what's with the towel?"

I choked back a laugh and used it to wipe my face. "Oh yeah. We need to talk about that."

———

Want more hot Daddies and their sweet boys? Jason needs a Daddy of his own, even though he's just bratty enough to self-sabotage things with any man who isn't just right for him. But Tony is persistent, and he fights for what he wants. Could Tony be the man to finally win him over? **_Find out in Have Mercy on Me._**